THE WILD ONE

THE WILD ONE

John Reese

A FAWCETT GOLD MEDAL BOOK
Fawcett Books, Greenwich, Connecticut

THE WILD ONE

Printed in the United States of America

11 10 9 8 7 6 5 4 3 2

Dedicated to another old Nebraska boy,
ROY SIEMILLER.

Chapter One

It was about 4:00 A.M. of a late spring morning when Henry Ely came out of the house, having eaten a quick cold breakfast without awakening his mother. The dogs came out from under the house to meet him, but when they saw he did not have a shotgun, they lost interest. He hurried past the windmill that supplied the house, past the smokehouse, the woodshed, and the first barn, to the corral where some thirty good horses pressed against the rails and pointed their ears at him.

Henry could not remember a nicer morning, and he had been born here in the Texas Panhandle and had scarcely been out of it in his nearly eighteen years. If he had finished growing, he would never be of more than average height. His shoulders, arms, and legs were thick. He did not look chunky, like his father, but he had Billy Ely's big hands and thick wrists and light-footed walk.

A row of saddles, covered with a tarp, hung on a hitchrail outside the corral. He removed his and set it near the corral gate. He was shaking the stiffness out of his rope when he heard his mother's voice behind him.

"Henry, where are you going at this hour?"

For the first time, he felt guilt. He lied to himself as well as to her. "Why," he said, "I'm going to fix some fence for the Riordans."

"For Mrs. Riordan, you mean. No, you're not."

"For the Lord's sake, why not?"

"I won't argue. You know it's not right."

"It's not? You tell me why it's not."

He turned finally to face her, dragging the loop of his rope impatiently in the dust. He saw a slender woman with a blanket thrown over her nightgown, and no shoes. He knew he had her light brown hair, blue eyes and fair skin, and his features were those of her father. Grandpa Gates was the person he loved best in all the world. If he had any love for his mother—and now and then he did—it was somehow for grandpa's sake.

The Gateses were from Rhode Island. Grandpa lived in Dallas, where he played and taught every instrument from the pipe organ to the mandolin. He had lost his New England accent, but Henry's mother had not.

In that accent she said, "I'm shamed to say it, but I shall if I must. Sarah Riordan doesn't want you to fix fence, and you look me in the eye and deny it? The time to stay out of trouble is before you get into it."

He said, "You should know."

She did not flinch. "I do know. I hope you feel better now you've said that, but if you think it excuses you, you're a liar in your heart!"

She accomplished one thing. She made him look the truth in the eye, although for her sake he did not confess it. He had a pretty good idea what was going to happen today, and he only hoped it would.

For a moment he loved his mother even more than he loved Grandpa. He felt the crazy Gates blood in him. He knew why his father had never understood her, and for that moment he was on her side.

It was said around here that Billy Ely had bad luck with his women. Bill's first wife, Isabel, mother of Henry's half sister, Natalee, had died of the typhoid. Natalee, now twenty-five, was married to Chris Pollard, and lived with him up on the Canadian river.

A second wife had divorced Bill the year of the big drought, but she was murdered by Kiowas before she could get out of the Panhandle, and Bill had buried her and mourned her as though the divorce had never happened. Less than six months later he married Eliza Gates. Henry was their only child.

When Henry was four, in 1874, Eliza ran off with a

railroad surveyor, taking Henry with her. Bill went after them, caught them in Kansas City, and brought his son back. Henry could remember liking the surveyor better than he did his father, but for some reason he could not remember his mother as she was then.

Bill took up with a young Mexican girl named Socorro. He had a child by her, Guillermo, before Eliza came back. Bill took Socorro and the baby to Abilene and bought them a little house and banked some money for them. Eliza left him again after a few months, this time to go back to her father. When Bill went to bring Socorro back, she already had another man, but she gave him Guillermo. When Eliza returned again, she brought the boy up like her own son, only she called him Billy. Billy was five years younger than Henry.

It had always seemed to Henry that his father could run anything but his own life. Henry had been ready to have it out with the old man, had he butted in this morning, but not his mother.

"I know the talk about Mrs. Riordan, Ma," he said. "All I can say is, by God nobody better say anything around me! She's the mother of my best friend."

"Don't you see? That's why you shan't go there today. How could you face Dexter—"

"Now Ma, don't accuse me of anything because I haven't done anything and I ain't going to do anything."

"Henry, you're a liar in your heart and now you've lied to me. If I *ask* you not to go, will you not?"

She almost sneaked up on him with that, but he remembered what was supposed to happen today, and he could not give it up if it killed him. The beating of his own blood made him say fiercely, "I promised to help them fix fence. Who's been complaining about their cattle all over our creek? I don't notice anybody in this family patching that fence!"

"It's not our responsibility, it's Frank Riordan's. He never takes care of anything of his," she said, with a scornful look. "But your mind is made up. Nothing I say will influence you.

"I guess not, Ma."

He shot a bar in the gate and leaned over to step

through it. He walked toward the fine horses that had retreated to the other side, and started them frisking in a circle around him. He chose a bay mare, one of Castle's get. He had forgotten Castle's book name. The horse had been a fine Kentucky stallion for which Bill Ely had paid twelve hundred dollars. The big stud was dead now, but no small part of Bill Ely's money had come from him.

Henry tried twice, but his hand was unsteady this morning. Both times the big mare ducked his loop. He knew his mother was still watching. Oh, the hell with everything, he thought, I'll ride Tom Monk. . . .

He crossed the corral, climbed through the bars again, and went to the second barn, which had stud-pens behind it. Castle's old pen was now occupied by his most successful son, Hidalgo, whose stud fee was a hundred dollars. Three other Castle studs—Saratoga, Telegraph, and Poland—gave service for fifty dollars each.

In the fifth pen stood the last colt Castle had sired, a big, brown, rawboned brute not yet three years old. A rattlesnake had killed this horse's mother when he was only a few months old, and he had been raised on cow's milk and a bottle. He showed no promise as a colt, but his personality reminded Bill Ely of a hired man he had had when Henry was a baby. The original Tom Monk, he said, had been too worthless to keep but too likable to shoot. Bill now thought Tom Monk might turn out to be worth something after all.

He was Henry's own horse and always had been. He stood like a horse with sense while Henry put a strong bridle with a curb chain on him, and he followed, docile as a house dog, when Henry led him to his saddle. He showed a little spirit toward the horses in the corral, but nothing a man couldn't handle easily.

Mrs. Ely had gone into the house. Henry rode north by west, and for a few moments gave Tom Monk his head. The horse loved to run, and the power he had in his gangling legs and the level seat he gave were beautiful. But he was only three years old and could still be spoiled. Soon Henry checked him to a trot.

And soon he began seeing cattle with the Riordans' Dot

X Dot brand, grazing with the Elys' own cows on Ely land. The damned shiftless Riordans, he thought. Too busy trying to get richer than us to take care of what they've already got. . . .

Which reminded him. He put his hand to his hip pocket and made sure of the wallet there. In it was $150, saved from the day wages he had earned since he was twelve. He and Billy owned livestock, in theory at least. Their father believed in giving sons a share of the increase. Cash money was another story. They were free to earn what they could elsewhere, when they were not needed at home.

But what had made Henry put the money in his wallet this morning? The same reason I rode Tom Monk, he decided. Claiming my rights. . . . But why was he claiming his rights today, instead of some other day?

He wished he had worn his gun today, too. Bill Ely forbade his sons to go armed, but it was Henry's own gun. He had paid for it. He wished he had his cornet, too. Grandpa had taught him to read music, and had given him the instrument. Now he missed it.

He came in sight of the Riordan place as the sun struck it. Somehow in his ear he could hear a cornet blasting the long, sweet, steady peal of an F sharp, and he shivered inwardly with an excitement he had never felt before. It was already the most wonderful day of his life.

Mrs. Riordan came to the screen door when she heard his horse. Somewhat to Henry's surprise, she was wearing a man's shirt and pants. She was a big-boned, wide-hipped, hard-working woman with strawberry-blond hair and freckled arms. Her eyes were green, her mouth stern and a little sneering. There was a lot of talk about her, but she was the mother of Henry's best friend, and he had never thought of her in that way until just recently.

The Riordans were an odd bunch, land-hungry but shiftless, anxious to be liked yet quarrelsome. There were two sons, Dick and Will, older than Dexter, and they were all alike.

"Well if you ain't stylish!" Sarah Riordan said when she saw Tom Monk.

"He needs the work," Henry choked.

"Well, let's see, you harness a team and I'll fill a jug and make some sandwiches. I believe we'll use Rowdy and Babe today."

He thought he knew all the Riordan harness horses. "Babe?" he said. "You got a new horse?"

"A pinto mare of Will's. I vow, they's more money wasted on fancy horses here! You harness up them two, and hitch them to the light wagon, and put the fence tools in it."

She went into the house, all business. She had always been more of a mother to Henry than his own mother, yet he never knew how to take her. Her dirty talk always shocked him, and lately it seemed she delibertately tried to make him blush, to show him he wasn't as smart as he thought he was.

But suddenly she had become just the mother of his best friend. He felt both shamed and disappointed, as he realized how much he had counted on something else.

Tom Monk began misbehaving as Henry rode him toward the ramshackle corrals among the cottonwoods, and when Henry saw the pinto mare, he understood. She was in heat today. He borrowed a strong halter from those the Riordans had hanging in a shed, and slipped it on Tom Monk under his bridle before tying him in the small barn. He harnessed the pinto and the sorrel gelding, Rowdy, and put the tools in the wagon.

Tom Monk was misbehaving in the barn, kicking and screaming his distress at not being able to get at the pinto mare. She was a sorry-looking excuse for a horse, Henry thought, but that was like the Riordans, they went for flash and style every time instead of quality.

Mrs. Riordan came out of the house, carrying a water jug and a basket of sandwiches. She said, "You ain't going to leave your colt tied in the barn all day, are you?"

Another time he would have explained why without embarrassment. Now he could not meet her eyes. "He's too damn mean today," he choked.

"Tie him behind the wagon, Henry. He'll kick the god-durn barn to pieces."

She climbed into the wagon and took the lines while he went to fetch the young stud. The horse made an exhibition of himself as he approached the harnessed team, and the pinto mare showed interest. Mrs. Riordan said nothing, but if she missed anything, Henry would have been surprised.

Somehow he was suddenly afraid of her, and he hated to get into the wagon with her. He tied the colt securely to the ring in the endgate and got into the wagon, and Mrs. Riordan handed him the lines. He spoke to the horses. The ill-matched team yawed widely, and the pinto mare tried to go up on her hind legs twice. He nipped her rump with the end of a line to make her behave.

"She is not what I'd call well broken," he said.

"Never been worked according to Will," Mrs. Riordan said, "but if she ain't a harness horse, she ain't nothing. Look at the goddurn fool! I'd as soon ride a bony cow."

"What did he give for her?"

She snorted. "I don't know, but if he gave more than forty dollars he overpaid."

"How's the spring grass up at the new place?"

"Real good, Frank says. He sent word by the mail rider that everything looks real good, but, shit fire, we can't take care of what we got, Henry. Four men on the place, and we'll be hiring by July."

They were out of sight of the house, and nearing the creek that, for miles, was the property line between the Riordan and Ely land. The pinto mare was misbehaving as badly as Tom Monk now.

A little willow-lined slough, scarcely half a mile long, ran down the Riordan land to the creek here. At this time of year the spring that fed it was flowing, the willows were in full leaf, and the grass was green. He walked the team slowly down the slope, looking for a place where the slough wasn't too mucky to cross.

Mrs. Riordan touched his arm. "Pull in here," she said. "Head them in so you can tie Rowdy to that willow yander."

He was choking again. "Why?"

"Let's breed that no-account mare to your colt, Henry. They ain't neither one of them going to behave until. I love to watch, don't you?"

She jumped out of the wagon. He glanced at her quickly

and dropped his eyes. "Well I don't know, now. He has only been stood a couple of times, and I don't know if I can handle him."

"Oh hell, you can handle your own horse!"

"Well damn, what if she hurts him?"

Many an eager, unskilled young stallion had been ruined for life by a mare that fought, but the truth was, Tom Monk was a gentleman about it, as horsemen said. He was the kind of easy going but bossy male that mares did not fight. But why waste him on that sorry spotted bag of bones, Henry thought. Why should I give the Riordans' fifty dollars' worth . . .?

"She won't hurt him! Do him good. Your poor horse, look how he's suffering! Ain't it the most ridiculous thing, the fix he's in?"

She was laughing—not just at the horse, but at all ardent male animals. He liked this less and less, but he did not know how to get out of it. He unhitched and unharnessed the mare, leaving only the bridle on her. Mrs. Riordan held her in the willows while Henry went for the young stud.

He unsaddled Tom Monk and hooked the curb chain of his bit to the first link. Seemed you could tear his jaw off with that bit, but the colt swung him off his feet when he untied the halter rope, and dragged him toward the willows and the mare. Oh Christ, he thought, I only hope she's not a bucker!

The mare was not a bucker. The coupling of horses was a wild, stirring thing to see, never the same twice, but Tom Monk was a gentleman. He came out of the willows tractable and at peace.

As Henry tied him to the wagon again, he heard the distant clanging of the bell on the Riordan's windmill.

"Frank and the boys must be home," he said.

"Oh my God!" Mrs. Riordan turned so pale her skin looked gray or blue under the freckles. "Hurry up! Hook up this mare for me, and then you git. Don't leave no tracks! Now let's see, I got to git out of this soft ground—get down by the fence to hard ground—only hope nobody backtracks me."

"What's wrong with you?"

She raged, "Well don't just stand there! Frank will kill you if he catches you here. The last thing he said when he left, you wasn't to hang around here. He's come back to catch us. I only hope he didn't bring the boys."

"Miz Riordan, I've hung around here since—"

"Bullshit. He's seen you looking at me!"

"You mean," Henry said, "he's seen you looking at me. I've got nothing to hide."

She slapped him. The heel of her big hand caught him in the eye. She had strength, and it hurt. She was saying furiously, "They'll see the wagon and tools is gone and they'll come straight here. Oh look! Yonder them calves—drop the fence and run them up here across our tracks. Then you git!"

"Those are our calves—"

"Yes, and if Frank sees them here, maybe he'll be so mad about it he won't suspicion nothing else."

The woman was crazy. She had been through this before, probably many a time, getting away with it more times than she had been caught, too. The calves were a quarter of a mile away, beyond the fence. Even if he could have driven them up here alone, the eight or ten of them would never obliterate the sign the horses had left in the willows. And any fool could tell that the fence had been deliberately dropped. Frank Riordan might be many kinds of a fool, but not that kind.

"Miz Riordan, all he has to do is go ask my mother. I told her I was going to help you fix fence today," he said.

"Oh, you tarnation idiot!" she moaned.

The bell clanged again—louder and longer, it seemed to him. He threw the saddle on the placid Tom Monk and cinched it tight.

"Ain't you going to help me hitch up?" Mrs. Riordan said.

"What's the good?" he said. "You better start thinking of something to say. Maybe you've got something to hide, but I haven't. The way it looks to me, you or Will or somebody owes me a fifty-dollar stud fee."

"You had better git out of this country," she yelled,

pointing her finger at him, "because they'll kill you if you don't. Although I don't know why I'm sorry for you. You sure don't worry about me none!"

He rode the horse through the muck of the willows, deliberately leaving deep tracks. He did not look back at the woman, but he knew she was hurrying to hitch up her team again. There's an experience I don't want again, he thought . . .

He was sure now what had been in Mrs. Riordan's mind today, and he did not know whether he was sorry or not that it had not happened. It puzzled him a little that she was so terrified of Frank, but as he became calmer, he thought he understood that, too. Frank could overlook what he could not help in most cases, but having it happen with Henry Ely was too much in the family. It was right under his nose and too almighty personal, you might say.

Safely back on his own father's grass, Henry dismounted to think it over. It would be just like Frank to come to our place and ask about me, he thought. The son of a bitch really hasn't got any shame. Maybe Ma would lie for me, but I don't want to stand there like a ninny while she does.

He slipped Tom Monk's bit and held him by the halter rope while the colt cropped the rich spring grass. Go ahead and stuff yourself, Henry thought, with a grin. You done yourself proud today, but I'm the one that gets the blame.

He was not afraid to go home, although he knew his father would disapprove of anything involving his family with Sarah Riordan. Any other woman, but not her. And old Bill would take it out on his wife. Henry could almost hear his father's cold, gruff voice.

"I don't know what you expected, Eliza. Where would he learn either self-control or taste? I suppose he will always be the victim of his passions, and so will all those close to him be victims. This is what you have never comprehended—that propriety is important. The boy will learn sometime, I hope, that there is a right way and a wrong way to do everything. But where would he have learned it by now? From his mother?"

There were some wild strawberries growing on the

south slope he knew about. He spent a good part of the day sitting there, slaking his hunger—at least a little bit—on strawberries and trying to understand how his life had been changed by the indecisive events of the day. It did no good to tell himself that nothing had happened. Here was a clear case of intentions being as serious as acts.

Toward sundown he mounted Tom Monk again and, circling his home widely, headed for Curtisville. He came down the wagon road into town considerably after dark, sparing the colt all he could. He did not intend to run from anything or anyone, but a fresh horse was always a good idea, just in case.

Chapter Two

There had been a school in Curtisville at the time of Henry Ely's birth, but it had closed for lack of money by the time Eliza brought Henry back to the ranch in the Panhandle. For a while she had taught him; but after the Riordans bought the adjoining property, Bill Ely proposed that they hire a tutor for their boys. Two other families joined the tutorial plan, although in the end, Bill Ely paid almost all the costs.

By the time he was fourteen, Henry had received a better education than most young men who then entered college. His speech remained the speech of the Panhandle, but he was not ignorant, and he had learned some of the arts of original reasoning.

The situation in which he found himself now, however, was so unlike anything in his experience that he did not know what he thought about it. He wanted to avoid trouble, having a conviction that if trouble were avoided long enough, Frank Riordan would lose his zeal for it. But one of the surest ways to fire up a weak and shiftless man like Frank was to run from him.

He felt a tendency to tremble that he supposed was the "nerves" that older people were always talking about. His experience had taught him what to do about nerves. There were two saloons in Curtisville. Behind the one where his father always stopped for his ceremonial one drink, there was a small stable. That would be the place to tie a colt which might be thinking, about now, of going back to find that pinto mare.

He put Tom Monk away and went into the saloon by the backdoor. The bartender was new to him. Bill Ely had taught Henry not merely the taste of whisky, but respect for it. He put a dime on the bar and called for his father's brand. The new bartender smiled.

"How old are you, fella?"

"Old enough."

"I think not."

"My name is Henry Ely."

The bartender sighed and poured the drink. Henry drank it without gagging and felt the bracing effect men talked about. Always before he had wondered where it was.

"Another one, Mr. Ely?"

"No thank you. One does me."

The bartender's face showed the relief he felt. "Like your father. I had me doubts, but when you're new to a town it's damned if you do and damned if you don't. Your father's a damned fine man."

Henry heard horses coming down the street at a walk. All he could see was their legs as they passed the window of the saloon. There were four of them, plodding along in single file. And if that wasn't the Riordans looking for Tom Monk, he would never trust a hunch again.

"Look here, I think those bastards are looking for me, and if they find me, there will be trouble," he said. "How about it, say you didn't see me?"

"You haven't been in," the bartender said.

"But if it's my father comes looking for me, I'll wait for him awhile back of the wagon lot."

He got Tom Monk out of the stable before the Riordans thought to look there. Behind it ran an alley, and beyond it was the lot where families camped beside their wagons when they came to town from a distance. Just as he led the colt through the wire gate around the lot, he heard the same plodding sound of more than one rider start down the alley.

Tom Monk heard it too. Henry got to his nostrils in

time, choking off the young stud's challenge. The four came down the alley at the same sedate gait, and they were the Riordans all right—first Frank, then Dexter, then Dick and then Will.

They were all armed, even Dick. It was too dark to be sure, but Henry thought that that old fool of a Frank had on two .45s.

He was more worried than frightened. There was no bedrock under Frank's bluster, but how to give him time for his righteous indignation to die down still had to be figured out. He waited until the Riordans were out of sight and then led his horse across the dark, empty lot. Behind it were some big cottonwoods. He waited there in the dark, standing close enough to Tom Monk to strangle any sound the horse might make at the wrong time.

He saw the Riordans twice again, making that stately parade down the alley, and he wondered why it did not occur to Frank to search the wagon lot. Maybe, he thought, Frank has had time to think things over. Maybe he is not so anxious to find me now. . . .

A couple of hours passed.

A man with a lantern crossed the lot, and by the rhythmic bobbing of the light he knew it was his father. Bill Ely had fought in the Union cavalry and had taken a bad saber wound in his left knee. When he was tired, that leg became unreliable.

"Here, Pa," Henry called softly. "Don't use your light!"

Bill blew out the lantern. "But nothing to worry about now," he said. "I saw the Riordans and you can bet they saw me."

"What did they say?"

"Nothing. You can bet they were mouthy enough to your mother, but Frank has had time to regret that. I told you, they saw me and they went home."

Henry sighed. "Everything is so goddamned simple to you, Pa."

"Simple in what way?"

"Get out of my way, here I come, ready or not."

"The Riordans are white trash. Here, I brought your gun, Henry."

So he was not going to receive any help from his father.

"Pa, that's exactly what I don't want! I am going away a few days, until Frank takes it out in jawing. If I ran into them now, they'd have to do something. But you know Frank is short on guts—and so are the boys."

"You don't have to hide from them. That woman—"

"I don't blame her. I knew what I was doing."

"I don't blame her. I have more respect for her than for Frank. I have expected this ever since you were fourteen. I never knew what to do about it and I don't know now, but I can handle any punishment due in my family. By the way, what did you do?"

Henry told him. "It didn't work out the way she planned—well, the way I planned either. She wanted that horse bred to Tom Monk, that's what she wanted."

"You wasted a Castle breeding on a Riordan cayuse," Bill said impatiently. "That's the Riordans for you. Frank, the son of a bitch, and his 'honor'! Well, we now have a price on it. Fifty dollars. That's what I'd get for a stud fee. But it was miserably managed, Henry. A man must be master of such a situation. In the relations between the sexes, we can learn from the higher animals, particularly the horse."

"Tom Monk was a gentleman, if I wasn't."

Bill nodded soberly, seeing no humor in his son's statement. He rarely saw humor in anything, and yet he was not a somber man or a quarrelsome one.

Bill was from Pennsylvania. He was teaching in a boy's school there when the Rebellion broke out. He helped raise a troop of cavalry and was elected lieutenant. After Bull Run he was a major. At the end of the war, he was one of Sheridan's best fighting colonels.

He saw four years of war without shirking his duty at any time. Even so he made money out of it, buying depreciated state bonds when things looked worse for the Union, sometimes at a dime on the dollar. He sold it all for par after coming to Texas to raise horses, when Congress funded the state war debts. His was one of the few Panhandle livestock properties without a mortgage on it.

Henry had no idea how much money his father had, but he knew there was a lot, although they lived simply, in a dinky little old house that had stood on the place when he bought it. He often wondered if his father might not have had better luck with his women, had he only spent a little on their comfort and pleasure.

"Come on home," Bill said. "Stay close to the house a few days until Frank cools off."

"No, there's Ma. I better let her cool off, too."

"She'll get over it."

Sure she will, Henry thought; only she was right. . . . He understood her better, suddenly. They were not quite civilized here on the Panhandle, or things like this could not happen. The existence of a woman like Sarah Riordan was an offense to his mother, and she had run away from all the Sarah Riordans as much as she had run away from his father.

"No, I'm going to take a little ride, I don't know where to."

"Wait until tomorrow, and I can get to the bank."

"I've got money, Pa."

"Not enough. You're not a saddle bum, Henry."

"Will you let me alone!" Henry burst out.

"I am merely trying to help you."

"Did I ask you to help? I got myself into this. By God, I'll get myself out. One thing is damn sure—I will not be managed like a kid any longer!"

Bill said, "I guess this moment always comes, with father and son. Now that it's here, I don't know whether to shake your hand, kiss you good-bye, or kick you in the ass. There's a wild streak in you. Don't let it get you into trouble. So long, son."

He hung Henry's gun belt over Tom Monk's saddle horn, picked up his unlighted lantern, and walked away. And that was that!

After he was out of sight, Henry wished he had asked his father to bring him something to eat. He was weak with hunger, but he did not want to waste the time and run the risk of eating at the hotel. He left Tom Monk tied to the cottonwood and went down the alley to the store, where he bought a ring of bologna, a piece of cheese, a sack of crackers, and some saddlebags.

He buckled the bags to his saddle. When he put the gun on, it did not seem to hang in the holster as it should. Investigating, he found his father had tucked four pieces of currency into the holster. There was enough light coming from the stars by now for him to see that each was worth one hundred dollars.

He put it in his wallet with his other money, mounted, and took the back way out of town. His only idea was to head north. He had been down to the border a time or two with his father, buying horses and cattle. He had never been thirty miles north of the house in which he had been born.

He ate as he rode. It was dry fodder, and he wished he had bought a canteen. First thing tomorrow—

It was then he heard someone coming behind him, riding hard and making as much noise as a runaway herd. He held the young stallion to a steady walk, although he had not much doubt as to who it was. On Tom Monk he could outrun any horse on the Riordan place. But while he would leave town to avoid trouble with the Riordans, he was damned if he would run for their pleasure.

"Hey, stranger—you seen five yearlings come this way? All bulls, crossbred Shorthorns. One's almost white, you couldn't mistake him."

Frank Riordan was looking for some of those scrubby halfbreeds they were always buying. For only a moment Henry felt relief.

But it was not time for that yet. They had blundered into him, and, because in his heart Frank did not want to see him and was not prepared to see him, it might be worse than ever. Here they came, all four of them, and Henry could not make himself kick Tom Monk into a run and leave them behind.

He felt a little sick as he wheeled the colt in the trail. Tom Monk had never been hard to handle before, but something about the day had changed him—maybe the pinto mare. He let out a blast to challenge all four of the Riordan horses.

"It's Henry!" Frank yelled suddenly in a high tenor voice.

Henry pulled the colt down with his left hand and held up his right, palm forward. "That'll do, that'll do! I ain't looking for trouble, but if I have to, I will shoot." One of the boys made a move behind Frank, and Henry raised his voice and said, "No, don't anybody try to get behind me. I'm not going to shoot unless somebody tries to pull some smart stunt like that!"

Through the dark he seemed to feel old Frank Riordan's uncertainty, his regret that blundering luck had brought a confrontation he did not want, and the blind rage he was deliberately building to see him through. Frank was a tall man, fleshless and bent from hard work that never seemed to get him anywhere. His drawling wit and mocking come-and-go smile made quick friends but not deep ones. A man could have sympathy for Frank now and then, but not much else.

"Why Henry, you thought you'd sneak out, did you?" came Frank's quivering voice.

"Go look for your yearlings," Henry said. "If you've got anything else to say to me, say it quick, because in about a minute I'm long gone from here."

"No you ain't. No you ain't!" Frank's voice rose to a thin squall that showed he finally had built up enough wrath to get him past this crisis. I'll give you one chance to pull your pistol, you little son of a bitch, and then I'm going to kill you in front of the boys you dishonored."

"You make me sick," Henry said. He turned Tom Monk so violently that the horse spraddled and almost fell. "Git!"

He saw only a blur of movement over his shoulder as the oldest boy, Will, fired at him. He was out of the saddle and on the ground as the slug screamed over him. He had gun-broken his colt himself, so at least he did not have a crazy horse on his hands. I should have shot first, he told himself. I trusted too much in whatever's the difference between an Ely and a shiftless Riordan.

Frank swore at Will and yanked off his hat to strike Will in the face before he could fire again. "Don't shoot him!" he screeched. "Get him and hold him for me."

"Yes, Daddy," Will quavered.

"Dick, damn you, he'p your brother!"

"Yes, Daddy!"

They both came at him and he still could not shoot Dexter's brothers. He released the reins and let Tom Monk run free. Henry charged at Will in the dark, pivoted at the last moment and lowered his head, and caught Dick in the stomach like a goat. Will slammed one at Henry's face that he could not entirely duck. It caught him in the forehead and jarred his wits loose for a second or two.

He went to his knees and wrapped his arms around Will's legs. He dumped Will on his back and fell on him, and his head cleared. Will was weeping and cursing, and scratching like an Indian with his fingernails.

Dick dropped on Henry from behind. Henry struck back with an elbow and caught Dick in the ribs, and Dick began weeping too. Henry came up with both knees and rolled backward, kicking out as he saw Frank leaning over him.

Frank's bootheel caught him in the mouth, and although he went blind again for a moment he did not go down. Frank was yelling. "Hold him, that's all. Can't the two of you handle him?"

Frank's boot came down again as both Will and Dick threw themselves on him. An explosion seemed to split Henry's head across the top, and he went limp. It was all right to quit now, he was thinking. There was nothing to do but quit.

"That's right, turn him over," Frank was panting, still in that high thin voice. "Hold the little sneak till I git my knife out!"

Pure horror cleared Henry's head. He sank his teeth into Dick's leg and brought a scream from him. He never did see Frank's knife, because Will smashed his fist down first in Henry's mouth and then on his temple, and he went floating off into the dark again.

He did not know when it was he came awake again, but it still was not over. Will and Dick were still sitting on him, and he could hear Dexter mumbling, in the frightened voice he always used with his father, "You ain't going to do nothing to him, Daddy. You put that knife away, you hear?"

"Dexter, you move aside," said Frank.

"You go plain to hell. Give me that knife, Daddy."

"I give it to you in a way you won't like. I gonna fix him so he don't invade no more homes."

Dexter began screeching too. "If you's half a man it nev-er'd happen. I tell you if you don't put that knife away, I'm gonna shoot you right in the Goddang guts!"

There was a noisy scuffle, both Dexter and his father cursing and crying. Dexter must have won it, because when Henry awakened it was almost daylight and he was still a whole man. They had given him the boots, probably all four of them, and he knew he was badly injured. But they had not gelded him.

He passed out again, and then next he found himself on his face, crying bitterly and trying to crawl toward his hat, which somehow seemed important. I can't do anything until I get my hat, he was thinking. I have got to get my hat on first. . . .

He got to his hat. Beside it was the gun he had not pulled. That was an error he would never make a second time.

The pain was too terrible to let him sleep, but he did rest. When full daylight came, he saw Tom Monk tied to a greasewood stem not twenty feet away from him. The Riordans' kindness and courtesy puzzled him for a long time. Then, as his head cleared a little at a time, he understood.

If Tom Monk came home with an empty saddle, Bill Ely would start asking questions, and he would know where to start. That was the kind of crisis Frank could not prepare himself to face. There was not enough raging wrath in him to ready him for that.

The colt was nervous, tired, and hungry. He was fighting the tie, and in time he would break his bridle and be gone. Henry got to his knees.

"You're about the ugliest horse I ever knew, Tom Monk," he said, "but you ain't going to get away from me. You wait, you ugly devil, you."

He lurched to his feet and almost screamed at the pain in his kidneys. It took him an hour to get to the colt and untie him and mount him. Tom Monk wanted to go home, but Henry turned him northward and held him down to a walk.

In a little while he saw five yearling bulls grazing beside the trail. One of them was almost pure white. A big sob burst from Henry, as he realized how close he had come to missing this nightmare. Had the worthless Riordans' cattle been a mile or two behind, they would have found them instead of him.

He wiped the tears from his eyes. And that's the last ones I'll ever shed, he told himself dreamily through the pain. No man or woman will ever hurt me this much again. I'll be the one who fires first.

The big ugly colt wanted to run, and he did not have the strength to control him. He wound his left hand in Tom Monk's mane and clutched the saddle horn with his right. The horse broke into a steady, rhythmic run, and Henry slept and awakened, slept and awakened, and slept again.

Chapter Three

A month later, when Henry Ely rode into Spade Rock, in the mountains of northern New Mexico, he was still passing bloody urine occasionally. His face had healed, but the beaten flesh under his eyes had scarred internally, changing the shape of his eyes. He had not shaved, and for some reason his beard had started growing coarsely. His face was covered with a half-inch of dark brown hair, through which his strong teeth shown whitely, changing the shape of his mouth too. He was not often free from pain.

He could not remember much of the past month. He had spent days in a sheep camp near the Texas-New Mexico border, lying in a Mexican hammock. He felt fine when he left there, but after an hour in the saddle he was in pain again, and stricken again with the fear that he would die here among strangers.

He was in the desert most of the way. Instinct made him struggle toward the highlands, where at least the nights were cool. In one town he bought a carbine, in another a skillet and a coffee pot. He rode the lonesome trails until he was gaunt as a skinned jackrabbit. When the pain was great, he could not keep anything in his stomach.

He had seen Spade Rock for half a day, a cluster of cubes on the west slope of the mountain. It looked larger from a distance than it did when he rode into it. Beyond the two he could see the flag flying over some kind of military establishment, but it did not seem to him to amount to much. The only people on the street were two middle-aged soldiers, sloppy looking, tough looking. They looked him over as though wondering if he had enough in his pockets to make a fight worthwhile.

"Where can a man sleep cheap?" he asked them.

"Mrs. Norton. The stone house, yander," one of them replied.

He managed to get off Tom Monk, but suddenly the pain hit, and he found himself trying to throw up from an empty stomach. He clung to his horse and waited for the agony to pass.

"Hung over a little?" said a voice.

He shook his head.

"Like to cash out that horse? I buy horses," said the voice.

His misery diminished enough for him to see a big man, well dressed in a black suit, good boots, and a fine white hat. He had longish yellow hair and a short yellow moustache, and eyes so blue they looked like glass.

"No thanks," Henry said. He still had more than four hundred dollars in his pockets.

"Give you a good deal on him. He looks like a good'n, and I don't try to cheat people."

I've got to get out of here before he talks me out of my horse, Henry thought. He started to lead Tom Monk toward the stone house, but a stab of pain, the worst he had ever felt, struck him over the kidneys. He felt his knees buckle as the world went black.

He felt the big yellow-haired man's arm catch him. "What's the matter, boy, you sick?"

"I'll be all right in a minute."

The man snarled at the soldiers, "One of you tie this horse and one go for the doctor. On the double!"

The soldiers obeyed—Henry knew that much, and then no more. He came to in a bed, with a ceiling over him. His pants were off, and he was on his stomach. Someone was gently pressing fingertips into his back, seeking and finding the sore spots.

"Someone give you the boots?" another voice said.

"They sure did."

"When?"

"I reckon a month ago."

"You can turn over and cover up. I'm through."

Henry turned over. There were two men in the room. One was the big yellow-haired man, the other obviously a doctor. The doctor was slender, dark, smooth shaven, and as handsome a man as Henry had ever seen.

"Bed rest," said the doctor decisively. "If there's no infection and he stays off his feet, he'll heal. What a country! They fight like animals. I suppose he's broke."

"No I'm not," Henry said weakly.

"A sick man doesn't need money in this town," the yellow-haired man said. "Can't you give him something for the pain, Doc? Paregoric, maybe?"

"I can, but that's tincture of opium, you know. It is a dangerous chemical, and I don't like to prescribe it."

"I'll see he doesn't get too used to it. Doc, you've never been beaten up this way. I have. The pain is not merely of the body. The soul needs rest too."

"Perhaps," the doctor said, "but the body is my jurisdiction. All right, I'll give you some opium. Keep him off his feet. Don't even let him go to the toilet! Have the old woman bring him the pot. I'll see to him day by day."

They both talked like educated men, but without any particular warmth for each other. The doctor left. The big man smiled at Henry.

"You heard your orders. My name is Keefe, Nevil Keefe."

Henry said the first name that came to his mind. "I'm Jack Neely."

"Texas, by your speech."

"Yes, sir. Mr. Keefe, don't worry about money. I can pay for my keep, if—"

"I can't afford to have you die on me," Keefe cut in smilingly, "because I mean to diddle you out of your horse when you're well. And you'll get well! You'll heal fast, at your age."

The man Keefe gave Henry—no, Jack Neely—a dose of paregoric, and he drifted away into pleasant sleep. Perhaps the drug worked on his soul too. When he woke up he was free from pain and ravenously hungry, and he was Jack Neely. When he remembered the Riordans, he seemed to see them stomping and kicking someone else, a kid he could not quite place.

For a week he swam in a pleasant paregoric haze, cared for by an old woman whose name was Mrs. Pepper. She was rude and resentful, but she brought him more good food than he could eat and she took care of his bed and clothes and brought him the chamberpot.

He was dreamily aware of visits by the doctor and Keefe. He did not know when they cut off the paregoric, but one morning he awakened with the first really clear head since that last attack. The doctor was standing beside his bed.

"Do you know me, Neely?" he was saying.

"Sure. You're the doctor."

"I would like you to see if you can walk now, if you will please. Tell me if you have any pain."

"I would like nothing better," said Jack Neely.

He could walk without pain. The doctor sent him back to bed, but allowed him to walk a little more each day. Keefe, he said, was out of town on a horse-buying trip. Henry and the physician became friends.

Dr. Joseph Littlejohn was a New Yorker who had come west to fight tuberculosis. He hated everything about the country, most of all being called "Doc" by strangers. "But I don't object to it from my equals," he hastened to add. "Among them, of course, I include yourself. I am sure you come from a cultured home."

Jack Neely held his peace. Whatever else he could call his home, it was hardly "cultured." Dr. Littlejohn went on.

"This is an animal environment. It's worse than animal. A human being fallen to the level of the frontier is lower than an animal. The noble savage of romantic European philosophy does not exist. He is a parasite upon the so-called lower orders, competing with coyotes, vultures, and other scavengers for the dead or maimed bodies or herbivorous creatures. The white man is even more objectionable. Keefe has the right idea. He is interested in these people only to the extent that he can make money from them. I would not want to be addicted to wealth as Keefe is, but it is better than any other reason I have heard for living here."

"I can't live off him forever," Jack Neely said. "One of those soldiers I saw when I came into town said that a Mrs. Norton, in a stone house, took in roomers. I can afford—"

The doctor cut in, "There is no Mrs. Norton. The soldiers were indulging their frontier wit at your expense. The stone structure they referred to is that most vital of frontier institutions, a house of prostitution. 'Mrs. Norton' is the trade name of a series of people who have operated it over the years. No, my boy, stay where you are until you're well! Believe me, Keefe can afford it, and if he doesn't talk you out of your horse, he will merely write the expense of your keep off to the cost of doing business."

The doctor pointed his finger at Jack Neely. "You must cultivate other forms of defense than fighting, especially if you're going to lose fights. There is no code of fair play here. Anything goes, if you can get by with it—and believe me, you'll get by with it if it works! For instance, whoever gave you the boots, and kicked you to the very edge of death—"

"That will never happen again," Jack Neely said softly.

Forbidden the saddle, he walked the town from end to end to regain his strength.

It did not take long. There seemed to him to be no excuse for a town here, and indeed there was none, since the hostile Indians who had made a military post necessary here had long since scattered. All that remained was a remount station commanded by an elderly lieutenant whose limited abilities were strained in merely keeping order among his riffraff troops.

The corrals of the remount station were almost always empty, Dr. Littlejohn said. The lieutenant had no judgment about horses. When mounts were needed, Keefe supplied them at the going market price. He was, the doctor said, a superb judge of horses and an instinctive trader.

The military reservation was known generally as Post Seven. The road to Post Seven passed the little stone house the doctor had explained. "Mrs. Norton's" place was set in a grove of pines slightly above the road. Jack Neely saw no signs of life there, in his walks about the town of Spade Rock, but he did not try to walk more than a few hundred yards from Keefe's house.

The largest building in town belonged to Chauncey Trimm. In a big locked room, Chauncey carried a stock of merchandise—simple necessities like beans, harness, men's clothing, tools, and ammunition. The rest of the lower floor was used as a bar and card room. Dr. Littlejohn shared Chauncey's room back of the bar, and they cooked their meals together on Chauncey's stove.

In the space immediately under the big flat roof were four small bedrooms that became the "hotel" in the fall, but that were empty now. Keefe's house was on the slope above Chauncey Trimm's place. There were two other ramshackle buildings on that side of the street, both empty since the reduction of Post Seven to its present status.

Across the single street of the town stretched Keefe's property. His big stone building contained barns for as many as forty horses, an office, and a tack room where a watchman slept. There were at least a thousand acres under fence, and corrals in which there were now more than sixty horses.

A long-roofed porch stretched the full width of Keefe's house. On the porch were a set of chairs with rawhide seats and a table on which a brass telescope always lay. From here, Dr. Littlejohn said, Keefe could train his telescope on anything that went on in Spade Rock.

One afternoon Jack Neely was sitting in one of the rawhide chairs when he saw Dr. Littlejohn plodding up the path from Chauncey's place. The doctor threw himself down on a chair without a word. Jack had learned that Doc had his moods. He was in one today.

"I guess Mr. Keefe will be back soon," he said.

"Today or tomorrow," the doctor grunted. "He sent in a string of horses today. He's usually not far behind them."

"I watched them come in." Jack touched the brass telescope. "Mighty good horses."

"Do you know horses?"

"I think so."

"Then you won't need to be warned to get all your horse is worth."

"I don't like to sell him at all."

"Keefe wants him badly. He'll have him as cheaply as he can get him. Listen! He told me once he figures to net five dollars on every horse he turns. I think he does better than that, but even at that price he's a rich man. And when you're dealing with a rich man, always remember he didn't get rich by paying top dollar. What do you figure your horse is worth?"

"I don't want to put a price on him. I—I wish I could work out what I owe to Mr. Keefe."

The doctor studied him squintingly. "How old are you, youngster?"

"Twenty-two."

"You're a liar."

"What's the difference how old I am? I can handle horses. I can break horses, and I've bought and sold horses. I could make a hand on a place like his."

"Jack, haven't you got a home to go back to?"

"No."

"Why did you get beaten up? It was over a girl, wasn't it?"

"We will skip that, Doc."

Littlejohn said angrily, "You can't detach yourself from life because of one bad experience. You're not just another ignorant cowboy. You have a future if you are capable of self-discipline—if you can go back home, and settle whatever breach of decency caused you to be beaten. Marry a good girl and—"

"No marriage for me!"

"What have you got against marriage?"

He had not thought of it in these terms, but now the words came boiling out, "In my family we have bad luck with women, if you have to know. My mother ran off with another man when I was small, and took me with her. Dad had to put another woman out of the house when he took us back. He has three kids, all by different women."

"An expensive hobby! I assume, though, that he can afford it, to judge by the horse you ride."

"He can afford it."

"Well," the doctor sighed, "there's a right way and a wrong way to do everything. We all have our little weaknesses, but they need not defeat us. Your father appears to have come to terms with his, and I only hope you may be so fortunate. I am fearful, however, that they addled your yolk when they beat you. You will be easily spoiled now. You have great possibilities for either good or evil, and this damnable frontier brings out the worst in all of us."

Go home? the youth asked himself, and his mind answered instantaneously, not by a damn sight! I will never go back there except to kill Frank Riordan, and he's just not worth killing. It was difficult even to think of himself as Henry Ely now. He was someone else now, a fellow by the name of Jack Neely.

A hint of movement on the desert slope far beyond the town caught his eye, and he picked up the brass telescope and rested it across the railing of the porch. Another string of horses, tied cavalry-style—nose to tail, was walking smartly up the wagon road. He counted fourteen head, and they all looked good to him.

Behind them rode a huge man who led a pack mule. It was too far to see the color of his hair, but it had to be Keefe. The quality of the horses said as much. He handed the telescope to Dr. Littlejohn.

"Keefe?"

"Yes," the doctor said, after focusing the telescope. He put the instrument down and stood up. "I will tell him you are a well man now. Physically, that is true, and beyond that I am not competent to testify."

Keefe was so far away that it took him an hour to reach town. Without the telescope, Jack saw Keefe and the doctor talking together as Keefe untied his string of new horses and turned them into a corral. I ought to go down there myself, the youth thought; but he felt a reluctance that was part shyness and in part the horse trader's instinct to make the other man come to him.

It was another hour before Keefe came up to the house. Jack was waiting for him on the porch. Keefe looked even bigger than Jack remembered him. He stood at least six-three and weighed at least 225 pounds, but he moved with the quiet quickness of a small man.

They shook hands, and Keefe smiled, crinkling his strange bright blue eyes. "Littlejohn tells me you're as good as new, Mr. Neely," he said. "What are your plans now?"

"First to get square with you, Mr. Keefe."

"Let's drop the 'mister,' Jack. My name is Nevil. How do you plan to square yourself with me?"

"You wanted my horse."

"I don't want your horse. You have four hundred dollars on you. How much do you think it has cost to keep you?"

Bewildered, Jack said, "He's a good horse. His sire was Castle, and in Texas a Castle horse is—"

"I know the Castle strain. You don't want to give him up, do you? Give up a horse like that and you decline among men. What's his stud-fee?"

"His half-brothers stand for fifty dollars."

"Let's say a hundred. I'll breed a mare to him and we're even. There are ranchers around here who fancy themselves horsemen. He can make you some money if you would care to stay around here."

"I would like to."

"Fine! Let's talk it over after supper."

But when they had sat down on the porch after supper, Keefe said, "If I were your age, do you know what I'd do? Go up on the mesa in Utah and trap some wild mares—a big herd! Take them to Wyoming or Nebraska or somewhere, and get myself a couple of big black Spanish jacks and start breeding mules. The Army needs mules all the time. So do the British. You could be a rich man in a few years."

Jack Neely had never liked mules, but he knew a vision when he saw one. He saw this one like a grown man. He said, "Someday, maybe. I—I am not ready for that yet, I reckon."

Keefe nodded. "I can use you here. I need a man to

care for things while I'm away, so my business does not wilt until I get back. I take it you're a horseman. Can you handle a gun?"

"I reckon so."

"If you only reckon, you can't—not well enough, anyway. I can show you a few tricks. You have big hands, and that helps. I'll pay you fifty a month to start, and you live here with me. If you make money for me, there'll be a commission. Suit you?"

"It's more than I expected."

"Let's hope it's not more than you're worth."

There was silence while Jack Neely drowsed over the vision of being his own man and making money—big money that his father would respect—someday. Somehow he could not *like* Keefe. The big fellow took himself too seriously. Even when he smiled his man-to-man smile, he kept you at a respectful distance, and you talked with him on Keefe's terms. But by God, Jack thought, he's giving me a chance, so I'll never be in a position where white trash like the Riordans can run me out of town.

Chapter Four

The heat had driven everyone indoors. The office was an oven, and even in the open barns the tied horses dozed hipshot, heads down, merely twitching their hides when one of the light hot breezes moved sluggishly through the building. A family of Indians—a couple and four children—had camped just outside the corral, near the road. For what seemed like hours, the only sound had been the fretful crying of the Indian baby.

Zwicky, the watchman and handyman (and the best horseman Jack had ever met) slept in a puddle of his own sweat on the clay floor in the corner of the office. Fowler, the bookeeper, an old soldier who fought a daily rearguard action against the liquor habit, dawdled at his books.

"Those five new horses Keefe brought in the other day, Mr. Neely," Fowler said.

"What about them?"

"How do I carry them? Trading stock? Surplus? Do they belong to some client, or what?"

"How do I know? I didn't buy them."

"He never bothers to tell a man."

"I've learned this, it's better to do it your way and make a mistake than bother him with detail. I'm going up to Chauncey's for a beer. Anybody want to join me?" Jack said.

Zwicky snored on. Fowler said, "I'm due for a bender, but let's put if off as long as I can. I wisht I knowed how to inventory them horses!"

"You're lucky to have something to do."

Jack went out into the burning sunshine. Things had never been in better shape here, and he knew it and was still discontented because there was nothing to do. Keefe had been gone for two weeks. If I had known how time would drag here, Jack thought, I don't think I would have stayed on for any money.

It was a mere two hundred yards to Chauncey's place, but he could not face the walk in this heat. He stepped to the window behind the office, where a stableman sat dozing with his head in his hands.

"Throw a saddle on that new gray," he said. "I'll sweat some of the ginger out of him."

In a moment the stableman brought out the little gray stallion, and held its head until Jack was in the saddle. Keefe had paid two hundred dollars for the horse over a month ago. He had been regretting it ever since.

The gray put his head down and took to the air. Jack fanned him with his hat and made him buck it out. It gave him no pleasure on a day like this, but he took note again that there was no distress over his kidneys.

The gray gave up. Jack loped him part of the way to Post Seven, teaching him his manners. He rode the horse back and tied him in the shade behind Chauncey's place.

"You don't stand this weather well," Chauncey said, as he set out a beer.

"It's doing nothing that drives me crazy."

"There is plenty of that here. Both doing nothing and being drove crazy."

Chauncey was a short, strong-looking, thoughtful man who kept his own counsel. When Jack did not answer, he went on, "In the fall it gets lively enough here for a while. Round-ups you know, and then the miners come down from the mountains, and there's still some trapping here and there. How do you get on with Nevil Keefe?"

"All right," Jack said.

His pay had been raised to sixty-five dollars a month. He had made a few trades and deals on which he supposed he had some commission coming, but he had never drawn any pay from Keefe yet. He had more authority and responsibility than Keefe had ever delegated before.

Yet when Keefe was away—which was most of the time—it was an unpleasant job, and he did not know why. People avoided him. Only Chauncey and Keefe's employees were civil.

"There is money to be made here," Chauncey said.

"Money's not everything."

"Show me something that'll take its place." Again Jack did not answer, and Chauncey again went on, "In the fall it's a right good place to be, and in the winter you may go to the Coast with Nevil."

"I don't know what you are getting at," Jack said, "but you're going to have to come straight at me with it. I am too hot and disgusted to reach."

"What I mean," said Chauncey, "is this: I'm as good a friend as Doc Littlejohn has got, but I'd say this in front of him. Don't let him poison you against Keefe. You've got a good job, kid. Take care of it!"

"He's not going to poison me against Keefe." For a moment, Jack's mind drifted idly. "He is upset because he thinks Nevil wastes himself here. He says Nevil could have amounted to something in a civilized environment. He claims Nevil killed a man here once."

Chauncey nodded. "He did. Some brush gunnie from the Rio Valley looking for trouble, and he got it. Don't let Keefe's soft talk fool you! It don't mean a thing. Things are so simple to Doc! Talk soft, act soft—talk hard, act hard. Why he don't—"

The back door opened and a man came in. He took off his hat and wiped it out with his bandana. "Man, it is some hot!" he said. "I bet there ain't a piece of ice closer than Santa Fe."

"Don't you bet there's any there, either," said Chauncey. "What will it be, sir?"

"Beer."

Idly, Jack looked over the man to whom Chauncey had said "sir." Well-built; slothful and sparing in his movements; small-featured, swarthy face that could have been carved out of brown rock. Wore a .45 with wooden butt-plates in a cutaway holster tied low on his leg.

And no doubt fancied himself dangerous. Jack had

seen the type before, riding past his father's place. None of his kind ever got work with Bill Ely.

"You own the gray stallion out back?"

It was the stranger, speaking to Jack. Jack said, "He's Keefe's. I work for Keefe."

"How old is he?"

"Barely three, we judge by his mouth."

"I suppose a man would bid against the cavalry if he took a fancy to him."

"He's too small for cavalry. He's for somebody who wants to breed cutting-horses."

The stranger nodded. "Yes, that short back, he looks nimble."

Jack felt his nerve ends tingle sluggishly. This was the way a deal started working. He said, "This fellow is set to turn in any direction, any time. You can't get him off balance. No sense yet because he has never been worked. But one week in a branding camp, and he is your boss horse."

"Stud horse in a branding camp? Ha! They're nothing but trouble."

"Not this fellow. He's a regular kitten."

"How high has Keefe got him priced?"

The tingle came on a little stronger. "Why for that matter, he's not for sale yet. Needs some lard worked off, and then Keefe will get his price."

"I asked you how much."

"Four hundred."

The stranger snorted. "He'll drag him off and bury him before he gets that."

"You could be right." Jack yawned. "He's a hell of a horse, but I like a bigger horse under me."

"Well, I'd be interested. But not at that money."

"Keefe will be back one of these days. Maybe he'd save you a buck or two on that price. I can't."

Long silence. "Mind if I try him?"

"Surely not. He'll buck some, but I reckon you could tie yourself on with your apron strings."

He and the stranger grinned at each other. The fellow went out the back door to try out the gray. Chauncey Trimm said, "Sure you want to deal with that *hombre*?"

"Why not?"

"You know who he is?"

"I know who he thinks he is. The Bad Man from Buzzard Bend himself and not an impersonation."

"He just about is. That's Dave Rogers."

"I still don't know who he is."

"One mean son of a bitch. They say he has killed five men. You ever meet a quick-draw artist?"

Jack said impatiently, "Lots of them. My old man used to just point his finger to get off the place, and that's all it ever took. Chauncey, this kind of saloon blather is what gives them a reputation."

"Maybe so. If you're wrong, it's your ass, not mine. But ask Keefe. Keefe is a fast-draw artist."

"I know he is. He works at it."

"And I wouldn't bet a dime on him against Dave Rogers. You shut up and live longer, Jack, and if there is a horse trade with Rogers, let Keefe make it."

"If there's a trade, Rogers will make it." Jack said. "I don't sell horses. I let people buy them."

He heard the gray stud coming back on a short rein, while this dangerous fellow, Dave Rogers, studied his short gait. He went to the back door to watch. Rogers had put his saddle on the gray. Now he traded back, putting it back on his own big black gelding.

Gunman or not, fast-draw artist or hot-air artist, he showed consideration for a horse. He said, "Too bad Keefe ain't here. I could like this gray horse."

"What do you want with him?" Jack said. "You've got a good horse."

"I'll make you a trade. My black will walk your gray into the ground and keep going till he breaks into a run. I paid two hundred for him a year ago, as a three-year-old. I'll swap you even."

"That's ridiculous, but talk to Keefe."

"Try my black horse!"

"No need to try him. We're two hundred dollars apart."

They dawdled. An hour passed. An hour and a half. After a little more than two hours, Dave Rogers gave his black horse and one hundred and sixty dollars for the gray.

Like Keefe, Jack now carried blank bills of sale in his pocket. Rogers could sign his name but could not read or write. Jack made out two copies, which Chauncey witnessed. Rogers left in a good humor.

"I'm heading for Idaho, and I'll ride by night until I'm out of the desert, Mr. Neely," he said. "By tomorrow morning, me and this horse will be friends. I think I skilled you with a shade the best of the deal."

"It has been done before," Jack said. "Good luck, Mr. Rogers."

The badman rode away, whistling between his teeth. When the sound had faded away, and they could again hear only the crying of the Indian baby, Chauncey said, "I take it something is wrong with the gray."

"No. He's just too small for a hard day's work. He'll play out easy, is all."

"You're just a smart-aleck kid. I don't mean Keefe wouldn't make the same deal, but he's in a position to back it up."

Keefe came home in the middle of the night, a week later. Jack heard the commotion down at the barn, and dressed quickly. When he got to the barn, Keefe had the big black gelding out in the middle of the corral, walking him on a long shankline and watching his leg action.

"Where did this fellow come from?" he said.

"Swapped the little gray stud for him and a hundred and sixty dollars."

Keefe whistled. "You just made yourself a fifty-dollar bill! Who'd you deal with?"

"Chauncey said his name was Dave Rogers."

Nevil cocked his head. "There could be more than one Dave Rogers, I guess."

"If the name means something to you, I guess this is the one. It meant something to Chauncey."

"And he stood there and let you deal that fellow out of his horse?"

"Well, he grumbled, but it wasn't his affair."

Keefe set the lantern down. "You headstrong little bastard, you haven't even got ordinary good sense!"

"I'm not bound out here, Nevil."

Keefe seized him by both shoulders and pushed him backward until he felt the wall of the barn against his back. "You miserable little fool! When I was your age, nobody took any trouble with me. I know what it is to be on my own, Jack, so you get this and get it good: so long as you're around here, you're not going to get killed by any gunfighter, and you're not going to turn into a gunfighter yourself."

"I don't want to be a gunfighter."

"You don't? Then listen when somebody tries to tell you something. Dave Rogers is crazy. The only fun he gets out of life is killing somebody and having people talk about it. Having people shut up and look down at the floor when he comes into the room!"

Keefe let go of him. Jack said, "I've seen those bit-and-a-half gunnies before. I've seen my pa order them off the place, and I've seen them go."

"But you have never met one who was *not* on your old man's place?"

"No, but—"

"You've done it. Tomorrow morning, gun practice—and I only hope it's not too late!"

Keefe got him out of bed at daybreak. They went up on the slope above the house, and Keefe had him shoot at bottles. He shot up a hundred .45 shells, and his wrist ached from the kick of the gun.

Keefe nagged at him. "Don't aim! It is *so* simple with big hands like yours. Slap your gun, make sure you've got your grip, now all you have to do is tip it up like you were pointing your finger, and squeeze off. You're not quail-shooting. Look, when a .45 slug hits you, you drop. Well then, you shoot first, and all you do is make sure you hit him somewhere. . . ."

Morning after morning they shot together. Jack watched Keefe draw and fire, draw and fire, draw and fire. I can't see that he's so fast, he thought. . . . But when they unloaded their guns and faced each other to shoot it out in pantomime, he always heard Keefe's gun click first.

Another blistering day, heat moving from the desert with no place to go. A peddler with a mule-drawn wagon stopped in front of Chauncey's place. There were a few

Indian families in town. From the office, Jack watched them cluster around the wagon. Then he thought he heard a brief, haunting wail of music.

That was all, a note or two. But it made him think, with a constriction in his heart, I wonder if he'd have a cornet, maybe?

He walked up to the wagon. The Indians made way for him, but a man and a woman were haggling over a pair of earrings with the peddler. The woman, he supposed, was one of the girls from "Mrs. Norton's place". The man was Truesdale, a soldier from Post Seven.

Truesdale was a big man with a stupid face, a massive chin, and the misshapen ears of a fighter, but he was not young any more. All Jack knew about him was that Chauncey's place was off limits to him because of trouble he had started years ago. He reached agreement with the peddler and paid for the earrings. He and the girl turned to go.

The girl saw Jack, and smiled. "Why hello there! You're Keefe's manager, ain't you?" she said.

She was not young either, but she was pretty and friendly, and her accessibility unnerved him. He mumbled something and pushed past her to the wagon. The peddler had no cornet, but he had a harmonica.

"No, that's not what I want."

"Please, not until you see it! This is not a simple mouth organ." The peddler held up the instrument. "With the valve open, it's all in the key of C, if you follow me."

"I follow you. No sharps or flats. That's what's wrong with it, you can't—"

"Please! The valve is worked with your thumb, deflecting your breath upward to the half note. Thus you have a full four octaves. With this you can play even symphonies. Try it!"

It was an instrument in size, if not in tone, and after he had the hang of it, the tone impressed him more and more. Dr. Littlejohn came up while he was trying to play a four-octave scale.

"I reckon not, thanks." Jack handed the instrument back to the peddler.

"I'll come down to fifteen dollars, sir."

Jack shook his head. Doc said, "I didn't know you were a musician, Jack."

"I'm not. I can blow a cornet a little but that's all."

"Oh, if you don't buy it, I'm going to buy it for you. If you can play music and won't, you ought to be lynched!"

Jack bought the harmonica, which came in a handsome case with a shoulder strap. He hung it over his shoulder and walked with Doc toward Keefe's house. He saw Truesdale and the girl in the street in front of Chauncey's place.

He did not know what had happened until he was on his knees. One knee hurt painfully; he had fallen hard. Then he saw Truesdale, and he knew the soldier had deliberately tripped him. The girl from the stone house had started to run, but she turned a dozen paces away to watch. And he thought, I'll be damned if I'm going to fight over her. . . .!

"Ignore it!" Doc was saying. "Ignore it, Jack. You can't compete with ignorance on its own terms."

Jack got warily to his feet and dusted off his knees. "Watch your feet, soldier," he said.

"You watch yours," Truesdale said.

Doc came between them and said to Truesdale, sharply, "If you must fight, find somebody else! This boy is just over a bad injury."

"Then let the son of a bitch stay out of the way with his big feet," Truesdale said.

Jack knew better than to take his eyes off the soldier, but in the background he seemed to see the girl from the stone house clearly. Her eyes were snapping with excitement. Her color was high, and there was something beautiful in the way she raised a hand to sweep a loose strand of hair out of her eyes.

He took three quick backward steps, unbuckled his gun, and handed the holstered gun and the harmonica to Doc. "All right, Truesdale, you seem to have something on your mind," he said. "Let's find out what it is."

By the way Truesdale came at him, he knew he was up against a skilled boxer who did not think this was serious enough to call for his best. Jack circled backward, trying to spin the soldier off balance. Truesdale kept groping for him with both hands.

Truesdale chopped at him with his left. Jack took it glancingly on his forehead, and the pain made him lose his wits for a split second; it made him remember so keenly the pain of the beating the Riordans had given him. He forgot the counterpunch he had meant to throw, as his legs went weak.

Truesdale brought up one knee. Jack dropped his arms around it and got a grip on the soldier's thick thigh. Truesdale was ready for this. He threw his weight forward and locked both arms around Jack's neck. Jack did not strain against the bigger man.

He went backward, keeping his grip. He heard Truesdale yell as he went on over Jack's head on his face. They came up at the same time, whirling to face each other, and to Jack the important thing was that there was no pain over his kidneys.

He moved in confidently on Truesdale, punching at the guts. He knew he was fighting a much older man, a heavy boozer, vulnerable internally. He took a few on his shoulders and head, but he got in a couple of good ones and then did not care that Truesdale had both arms locked around him.

He kept punching at those guts. Truesdale lifted Jack off his feet. Jack brought his knee up dead center in Truesdale's crotch. Truesdale dropped, and after that it was easy.

Now he had only to move inside and stay there. He beat the soldier's guard down and then measured him. He caught him as he came in, and dropped him with a right that should have torn his jaw off. Truesdale did not lose consciousness, but sat down, reeling on the seat of his pants and rubbing his bloody mouth.

"I'll be a son of a bitch!" he said, without heat. "The next time, kid, I'll whip you."

"The next time I'll knock your brains out with a club," Jack said.

He buckled his gun around him again, but he did not hang the harmonica around his neck. The woman from Mrs. Norton's place followed him with her eyes, her face falling as he ignored her. Just seconds ago he had been fighting over her, but now she aged shamefully without knowing what had happened.

What had happened was that she reminded him of Mrs. Riordan, and he wanted to run. Doc fell into step beside him, saying, "You're a savage, too. That poor stupid soldier!"

"What do you want me to do—run from him?"

"It is better than descending to his level."

"When do you stop running, Doc? What happens if he corners you finally, and you can't run? Do you turn the other cheek?"

Between his teeth the doctor said, "You get out of this miserable environment before you become a part of it. The brute rules here excuse nothing! A civilized man belongs in a civilized country."

Jack tried to outwalk him. "Doc, you get on my nerves. Let me alone."

"I will not let you alone! If you won't listen to me, listen to Keefe."

"I do listen to him. He's teaching me to shoot a gun."

"Ha! Savages like Truesdale leave Keefe alone because they know he'll kill them if they don't. That is one way to rise above your environment—to be fast with a gun."

"I am fast."

"Not as fast as Keefe."

"No, but I'll be faster."

They had reached Keefe's porch. Doc said, "By the lord, Jack, I'm afraid you may be, and I am truly sorry for you, boy!"

"Don't be sorry for me."

"I already am. I saw your face when you were chopping that soldier-beast down. Given skill with a gun, in addition to what you can do with your fists, and there are no depths to which you cannot sink. Jack, I wouldn't want to live the life you're going to live until you're my age—if, that is, you last that long!"

Jack put his hand to his forehead, which throbbed from

that first glancing blow of Truesdale's. "I'll last," he said, "but it's a hell of a world, isn't it?"

"If you know that, you're not a kid anymore, Jack. And I believe I pity you with all my heart!"

Chapter Five

"That is *so* pretty!" said Mrs. Pepper, Keefe's housekeeper. "What do you call it?"

"It's a march," Jack said. " 'Seventh Regiment Bluejackets,' I think."

He sat on the bottom step of the porch, wishing the old woman would leave him alone. It was a chilly night, which showed that autumn was not far away. There was a full moon, and inside him a restlessness and an ache that nothing could assuage. Months had gone by since the fight with Truesdale, yet at times—tonight, for instance—he could see clearly the face of the woman who had caused it.

No good telling himself she was just a hooker from the cribs, an enlisted man's whore. If not her, he thought, then why not some other one? Or are they all like her and Mrs. Riordan?

" 'Lorena,' " Mrs. Pepper sighed. "Do you know that one? My family was Reb. My brothers, I remember them singing it."

"I learned that one on the cornet, too. Do the best I can, ma'am."

He leaned back and put the harmonica to his mouth. It wasn't the instrument a cornet was. A man couldn't get the power out of it that there was in a horn with a bell, but it had points in its favor, too. He liked fooling with harmony on it, something you couldn't do on a cornet. You could play accidentals too, which gave you a chance to improvise a little. You could slur and play a *glissando* about as well as you could with a cornet, and—

Mrs. Pepper got up and silently faded back into the house, and he knew what that meant. He dropped the harmonica in his lap as Keefe came plodding wearily up the path, carrying two big suitcases.

"Was that you playing, Jack?"

"Yes. Just a harmonica."

"You've got an audience down on the street, did you know? Everybody in town, and half of Post Seven. What was that you were playing?"

" 'Lorena.' "

Keefe's strong white teeth flashed a smile in the moonlight. "You'll have some of those Southern boys crying into their pillows tonight. Play some more."

"I don't feel like it."

Keefe put his foot on the bottom step beside Jack, without putting either suitcase down. "I didn't know you were musical. I didn't know you had the instrument."

Jack looked off into the darkness and said, "I didn't know I had to report to you everything I do."

"Do you read music?"

"I used to."

"You're a plumb artist, to be sure. All right, professor, I'll ask you—will you kindly favor us with a tune?"

You just got to where you could shoot the overbearing bastard in the back, and he said something that left you like a dog with the tin can of your own small nature clanking on your tail. Jack played the old Southern love song again. Keefe asked for the march he had played before, and again Jack played "Seventh Regiment Bluejackets."

"Do you know you were playing thirty-seconds?" Keefe said.

"It can be done on this peanut whistle."

"Where did you learn music?"

"My grandfather teaches it. I'm not a hundred percent ignorant."

'You should have said something. I've got a pretty fine violin in the house."

"I never touched a violin in my life."

"If you can get that kind of music out of a harmonica, you can play a violin. I wasted some of the best years of my life trying to learn it, but music is something you either can or you can't, and I can't. I'll go get it."

He went bounding into the house with his suitcases. Jack heard him fooling with the violin a long time before he came out of the house, saying, "I had to restring it. I can teach you the fingering and the bowing, but I would play hell teaching you anything about music."

"I don't want to borrow a good violin."

"You're not borrowing it. It's yours."

Jack shook his head. "I can't take a present, Nevil, and I can't afford to buy it. And I never wanted to play the violin anyhow."

Keefe stood there with the instrument in his left hand, the bow in his right, and on his face the look of a man who has lost his best friend. Why, this means something to him, Jack thought. He's mightily stirred up about something . . .

"A violin scares me to death, Nevil. The prince of instruments, my grandfather said. Give it to someone who can play it."

"How many musicians do you think come through Spade Rock? I'm too tired tonight, but tomorrow I'll start teaching you what I know."

Jack took the violin, tried his fingers on the strings, and then got up and put it on the table without trying to play it. He did not need to be told that it was an exceptionally fine instrument, and very old.

Keefe stretched out in a chair and kicked off his boots. "I had a hell of a trip."

"Where'd you go?"

"San Francisco, Sacramento. And listen—I matched up four pintos on the way home. Two three-year-olds and two four."

"Are they any good?"

Keefe shrugged. "They're pretty. See if you can deal them off so I won't have to feed them all winter. I'm in five hundred and twenty dollars."

Pintos, like palominos, buckskins, roans, red chestnuts, and blacks with flashy white points, were premium horses.

But you paid for looks, and looks might be all you were getting.

Keefe did not ask how things had gone in his absence. In a few days he would find time to go over the books with Jack and the bookkeeper. It never took more than a few minutes. A curt nod or two, and Keefe had approved every judgment Jack had made in his absence.

The next day Keefe gave Jack a violin lesson. He brought out a music stand and a big chest of sheet music. There was a swift, finicky sureness in the way his big fingers fled over the bridge, yet it was clear that he did not have the music in him. He lacked the power on the violin that he had with a horse, a gun, or a deck of cards. It had no enchantment in his hands.

In Jack's it did. He put the harmonica aside and worked an hour or two every day on the violin. Keefe went away again, this time up into Colorado for a last trip before snow closed the high passes.

By the middle of October, Spade Rock was busier than Jack would have dreamed possible last summer. Hands were drifting down from the north—from Saskatchewan and Alberta, Montana, and Idaho. Many of them had their summer's wages on them, and there were jobs for a few around here. The roundup here was a month earlier than in the Texas Panhandle, and cattlemen were hiring.

Every cowboy with money in his pocket broke his heart over the pintos Keefe had bought, and one who had won three hundred dollars in a poker game offered all of it for just one of the horses. But to make a few dollars on one horse was not enough, not at the expense of spoiling a matched pair of pairs.

In the evening, Jack practiced the violin in the office. It was always warm here, and the larger room gave the instrument a better tone. Zwicky puffed his pipe and dreamed, neither a distraction nor an inspiration.

One evening Zwicky was not there, but he came in a few moments after Jack started playing. By his look, he was agog over something. Jack put down the violin.

"What's up?"

"Jack, there's a rich Chicago lumberman in town. He's

took all of Chauncey's rooms he could get. He's scouting timber with a guide, a cook, a wrangler, and a feller with glasses and a moustache that's his secretary. They want to put up nine horses here."

"Why sure, we've got room."

Zwicky grinned. "Sure, but the idee is, the fella that's wrangling their horses asked about them pintos. I think that rich feller likes them, and I reckoned you'd like to get shet of them horses before Mr. Keefe gets back."

"Did you get the lumberman's name?"

"Barr. Jonas Barr. You want I should start gentling them horses tomorrow? They's barely halter broke."

"No," Jack decided. "Let's play a pat hand. Make him pay to look."

He had lost interest in the violin, but he waited until after 10:00 before going into Chauncey's place. It was packed tonight. Time had been when he would have felt diffident about pushing through a crowd like this, at his age. Now he simply did not care. With Keefe out of town, this was his Spade Rock, and they better know it.

Chauncey beckoned to him. "There's a fellow by the name of Barr in town who is interested in Nevil's pintos," he said. "You might want to be introduced to him."

"I reckon not. Nevil's got big plans for those circus horses."

Chauncey looked at him queerly. "Well, I told him I'd send you up to him. What I'll do is send up and tell him you're here. He won't like that. He's an unsociable booger."

Jack watched a poker game for an hour. Then he heard his name being called. Chauncey was beckoning to him from the bar. Beside him stood two strangers, obviously the lumberman and his horse wrangler. Jack again made his way through the crowd.

Barr's handshake was barely civil. "I'm told you're in charge of those four spotted ponies in the public stable, Neely," he said. "How much are you asking for them?"

You're really used to having your own way, for a fact, Jack thought. . . . Mentally, he came up on his toes and cocked his left. He had a sudden feeling that this was one of those shining, luminous, fill-or-go-broke moments that hit a man only once in a lifetime.

"If you mean Keefe's pintos," he said, "they're not for sale."

"We can eliminate the maneuvers. Everything is for sale."

"That's right, but there's a time and a place. Nice to have met you, Mr.—Carr, is it?"

Barr flushed and followed him through the crowd. "Don't get on your dignity, Mr. Neely. I am interested enough in those ponies to pay a good figure for them."

"They're not ponies. Come see me in two months, Mr. Carr."

"Barr."

"Sorry. Those four are one of Keefe's speculations, and he has a habit of cashing in on his long shots. You just called them ponies. Let me tell you something about a pinto horse. And it's *horse,* Mr. Barr.

"A pinto doesn't make his full mane and tail until he comes on five. The older and fatter they get, the handsomer a pinto is. This is why you can't buy them now, sir: you can't see it in them, but there is five thousand dollars in those four horses. That's what they'll bring in two years, after they've got their looks and are broken to harness."

Barr laughed. His wrangler had come up behind him, and now he said, "Mr. Neely, if there's a damn fool here, it's not Mr. Barr or me. I can buy a horse like that anywhere for from two hundred to two-fifty."

"And you can buy four matched ones for about a thousand, if you want to spend a year doing it," Jack said, nodding. "These are two of the showiest carriage teams in the world. Keefe will take them to Chicago or St. Louis, and exhibit them in silver-mounted harness. He will get two thousand dollars for the first team he sells.

"And then the fellow who buys them is going to come back, probably the same day, and pay *three* thousand for the other team, rather than let somebody else have a turnout that equals his. He'll be some man with a wife and grown daughters who already have everything else. He'll put a coachman and a footman in livery on his carriage.

You picture that man's womenfolk going to church on Easter morning now, will you?"

Jack tapped the wrangler on the chest, ignoring Barr. "New clothes all around. Flowers in the vases, and the side-curtains down. Silver-mounted hames and silver-plated bit rings. Harness freshly blacked, and pom-poms on all four headstalls. Those four fat pintos oiled till they shine. Now you tell me whether Keefe is going to get five thousand for them or not!"

Barr followed him outside. Dr. Littlejohn passed, and Jack introduced him to Barr and then stood talking sociably with the doctor. He knew that Doc sensed something without knowing what it was. Inside, Jack's nerves were singing like the E-string on his violin, but he felt he had his nine, ten, jack, and queen of a suit, and had it open at both ends.

"You must excuse me, gentlemen," Doc said gravely. "I have to attend a patient."

Barr said, "Let's go look at those horses again, Mr. Neely."

An hour later, they signed a contract for four thousand dollars, the horses to be delivered in Chicago at Barr's expense, within six months. Barr counted out two thousand dollars in brand new hundred-dollar gold pieces to close the deal. Barr took one last look at the four pintos and then went back to Chauncey's place, followed by his stupefied wrangler.

Half a minute later, Dr. Littlejohn came in. Jack picked up the stack of gold pieces in both hands, and let them jingle down on the desk.

"The pintos! Keefe will drop dead, and this is just half."

Doc sat down and counted the money rapidly with his fingertips. "You've gotten used to winning, Jack. You're not the raw boy who came in here all kicked to a pulp."

Jack stacked the gold pieces again. "I hope I'm not. That's one of the places I learned that the difference between winning and losing is holding your nerve at the right moment. I lost that one, when I got beat up. I'll never lose another one."

"And you're still not happy."

Jack stared into the winking eye of the draft in the

stove. "I don't know what it takes to be happy, and that's the truth. I'm not happy now, no. But nobody is ever going to stomp on me again!"

He put the money in the safe, and they walked to Chauncey's place together. In front of it, Zwicky stood holding a saddled horse. "Mr. Keefe's back," he said. "Just rode in. Went inside to have a drink."

"I've got news for him," Jack said. "For you too, Zwicky. I sold the pintos."

He went inside with Dr. Littlejohn at his heels. "You won't be telling him tonight," Doc murmured. "He has found himself a game, his kind of a game."

Jack had never seen Keefe play poker, but he knew his reputation. He watched the game for a while. Keefe was losing, dribbling money away in pots of two and five and ten dollars. He looked fat and sloppy, sitting there with his coat off, his shoulders hunched, and the collar of his travel-stained shirt open.

Keefe had lost around fifty dollars when Jack went home. When he got up at daylight, he could see from his bedroom window that horses were still tied around Chauncey's place. The game was going at the same quiet tempo when he got down to the barroom, but there was a difference: the other games had stopped and the entire crowd was watching the play at Keefe's table. Jack had to stand on the rung of somebody's chair to watch from thirty feet away.

To judge by the stack of chips and cash in front of Keefe, he had a long streak going. Keefe still had that sleepy, dull-witted look on his face; yet Jack sensed something different. A man playing a streak the way a streak should be played had a sort of rapture. His mind raced ahead of the cards and his nerves outran his mind. No man knew how to read another man's mind, but at times like this, something like that happened.

A man whose back was to Jack stood up. "How much of my paper do you hold now, Mr. Keefe?" he said.

"I think about four hundred, sir," said Keefe.

"You're too much for me tonight. Can I pick up those notes next week, when I'm back from Albuquerque?"

"This paper is like gold to me. You may have it back whenever it is convenient."

"Thanks, Keefe. I'll never play with you again, but tonight was worth what it cost me."

The man stepped aside. Another man slid into the empty chair. Keefe looked at him dully, and then a flick of something crossed his face.

"We don't sit down armed, Mr. Rogers," he said.

Dave Rogers! Jack could not remember the gunman's face, but he recognized it when Rogers stood up to shuck his gun and hang it on the back of his chair. He sat down again.

"Ante a dollar?"

"That's correct, sir," said Keefe.

"That baby-faced kid still work for you?"

"We're playing a game of cards here, sir."

"Yes. Yes, but you tell him I want to see him tomorrow, Keefe."

The man with the deck pushed his hat back and wiped sudden sweat from his forehead. They were playing dealer's choice, no wild cards. It seemed to Jack that he was having trouble making up his mind to stay in the game with Rogers.

Yet he could not make himself get up just because the gunman had sat in the game. "Little hand of draw," he said. "Are we all in?"

Rogers caught the cards that came skimming to him and slid them under his left hand. "You be sure and tell him, Keefe," he said. "You tell that little son of a bitch that him and me owe each other a little talk."

Keefe waited until the hand had been dealt. He stopped the game with a look and said, "Mr. Rogers, don't interrupt the game again for any purpose, and don't try to give me orders at any time, if you please."

"Well, excuse me!" Rogers said. "We are some touchy, ain't we?"

"We are playing cards."

"Then let's play cards, but that kid skinned me on a deal and I am going to have my money back or his hide, and I don't much care which."

Keefe stood up. "If you must, you must, I suppose. Jack Neely works for me and I handle all complaints. What is bothering you?"

Rogers stood up too. "He stole my horse. He swapped me a runty little gray stud and took my horse and my money."

Jack tried to push toward the table, but too many men were suddenly pushing away from it. He heard Keefe say, "You're not the first man to bellyache because he beat himself on a trade, but I never before saw one whine like a dog about it in a public place. Suppose I meet you out in the street in five minutes—?"

Jack heard Rogers call Keefe a name. The crowd parted in time for him to see Rogers take a long, thin knife out of his shirt front, holding it with its short butt against his palm. Rogers leaned forward like a striking snake, and Jack thought he heard the thud and rasp as the keen blade went through Keefe's breastbone to the hilt.

Keefe screamed, twisted, and fell face down on the poker table. The point of the knife broke through his back, blood bubbling around it. Rogers snatched up his gun from the back of his chair and made for the door, holding the holstered gun in both hands.

Jack jumped up on a chair and yelled at him, "Rogers, you yellow son of a bitch! Wait for me outside somewhere."

He was not sure if the gunman heard him. Doc and Chauncey tried to hold him. "Listen to me!" Chauncey babbled. "This is an old stunt with him. He'll make you draw first. He'll kill you in self-defense—"

"He never saw the day he could," Jack said.

He gave Chauncey an elbow in the belly and put the palm of his hand across Doc's face to push him aside. The floor of the suddenly empty room echoed hollowly as he ran toward the door. At the door he stopped. The street was in full sunshine now, what he could see of it over the backs of the restless horses tied here.

He stepped outside. No sign of Rogers anywhere. Jack had never felt as sure of himself. What he had in him was probably like the rapture of self-confidence with which

Keefe had played poker all night. Maybe he was fooling himself. But let's find out, he thought. If I am, I won't have long to regret it. . . .

He stepped down into the dust. One by one, with his left hand, he untied eight horses from the rail in front of Chauncey's place. Hungry, stiff with cold, they scampered away, leaving him a clear view of the street. Still no Rogers. Jack walked slowly out in the middle of the street. The one thing he did not fear was a shot in the back. There were enough guns around here to riddle Rogers like a sieve if he tried that.

Where was the big-mouthed knifeman? And somehow Jack knew. Rogers was waiting for Jack to call him a yellow son of a bitch again, to get him mad enough again. Well I won't do it, he thought. I have got it won already. I can wait.

He waited.

Rogers came out from behind the corner of Chauncey's place, and had Jack not turned the horses loose, they would have been between him and Rogers now. Jack cocked his head and watched Rogers, and he knew he had been right and all the rest of them wrong. A badman was just a crazy man who had been lucky a few times. A poolhall sport who could shoot a little, but who had to nerve himself to do the job that earned him all that spooky gossip he enjoyed so much.

Rogers took two slow steps toward him. Jack said nothing, did not move, did not smile or sneer or help warm up the guts that had gone cold inside Rogers. One more step. Another.

Rogers went for his gun first.

As Keefe had said, it was *so* simple when you had big hands! Jack slapped the gun out, hooked the hammer, tilted the weapon back with the butt in his side, and squeezed off a couple. Keefe was right about another thing, too. Anywhere a man got hit with a .45 slug was good enough to down him.

Jack's first shot caught Rogers in the lower belly. His second one smashed in Rogers's chest. Rogers was flung backward with his gun in his hand, like a half-emptied sack of flour. He did not move.

Dr. Littlejohn came out of Chauncey's place and knelt beside Roger's body. He felt for a pulse, for any sign of the life that had been hammered out of him by those two big pieces of lead. He turned back Rogers's eyelids and stretched out to put his ear on his bloody chest. When he got up and looked at Jack, his bloody face was full of hatred.

"You finally got there, didn't you?" he said.

Chapter Six

Jonas Barr was at the office in an hour. Jack and Doc had been sitting there with their thoughts, not trying to talk it out until both had cooled down. Doc got up and let the lumberman in.

"This leaves me in a questionable position," Barr said. "Surely the deal is off?"

"I don't see why," Doc said, after Jack waited to let him answer. "Mr. Neely was authorized to make the deal. The court will surely appoint him to carry out this and other pending contracts."

"But probate is a long process. You know as well as I do that probate-dispersal prices are lower than the average market. I'm willing to take the ponies, but I feel the amount I gave as a binder is all they're worth now."

Jack nodded, and before Doc could formulate an answer, said, "Certainly, sir. Bring me your bill of sale and I'll give you back your two thousand in the same gold pieces. I'll take the pintos for what Keefe owed me. Go tell them good-bye now, if you like."

Barr wanted to argue, but he wanted the pintos worse. Within two hours he was on his way out of Spade Rock with his little caravan.

Keefe and Rogers were buried at the same time, with the lieutenant from Post Seven reading a service from some field officer's handbook. Chauncey walked down to the street with Jack.

"Wonder if anybody realized we were burying the town of Spade Rock, too," he said.

"I did. How long will it last now?" Jack said.

"Until the Army abolishes Post Seven after it finds out it can't get any more horses. Oh, I'll make out! I may do even better than in the past. The truth is, if there was any money to be made, Keefe made it. Now I'll get a few hogs. The Indians raise enough corn to fatten them, and I'll sell meat and groceries. I'll lay in a stock of women's goods."

"Any place you can get fresh pork is getting too civilized for me," said Jack.

Doc was waiting for them in the office with Fowler, the bookkeeper, and old Zwicky. Jack said, "He never knew I sold the pintos for him. I wish he could have known that."

"What will you do about them now?" Doc asked.

"If it's up to me, I'll have Zwicky break them and deliver them to Chicago. It was his deal. He's entitled to some money out of it too, I'd say."

"He surely left a will."

"In the safe, I think," Chauncey said. "He had a personal drawer inside it, didn't he, Fowler?"

Fowler opened the safe. They opened Keefe's personal compartment with a key taken from his body. On top of the little stack of papers was an envelope marked, "*Last Will and Testament of David Nevil Keithly, a.k.a. Nevil Keefe.*"

Doc opened the envelope. The will had been drawn up by a Santa Fe attorney and attested by a Notary Public. It consisted of a simple line. *Everything of which I die possessed, after payment of my just debts, I bequeath to my wife, Yvonne Laura Keithly, born Yvonne Laura Blanchard.*

"Logical!" said Doc. "I was sure it wasn't his real name. He was really two men."

In another envelope, marked simply "Yvonne," they found Mrs. Keithly's San Francisco address. They also found money order receipts, some fourteen years old and some dated less than four months ago, that added up to eighty-five thousand dollars.

"Over six thousand a year," Doc murmured, "and he

spent plenty on himself, too. When he went to the Coast he lived in style, and he was never short of cash for an investment. It had to come from somewhere."

More envelopes revealed deeds to two business buildings in Sacramento and one in Reno, and a deed to a ranch in Nevada. Bank books showed total deposits of fifty-thousand dollars in banks in Reno, Sacramento, Stockton, and San Francisco. He owned stock in the ones in Stockton and San Francisco, and he owned a 40 percent interest in a new San Francisco hotel. The most surprising find was a document showing him to be half-owner of the ship *El Cid*.

"Why, I've seen her!" Doc said. "She's worth a lot of money and she's a big money-maker in the China trade. "Nevil must have been worth close to half a million dollars altogether. We haven't found it all, I'm sure."

No wonder, Jack thought, that he never had time to start that mule-breeding ranch. . . .

That afternoon, a United States duputy marshal rode into Spade Rock. He swore Dr. Littlejohn, Chauncey Trimm, and the lieutenant from Post Seven in as witnesses, and they opened Dave Rogers's grave. They exposed him to sunlight and then buried him again.

Rogers, the marshal said, had robbed a Utah post office. He was looking for a shipment of currency, and had expected five thousand dollars. He got less than a hundred and fifty, and he killed a mail clerk. The clerk was a Mormon, and the Saints had put a thousand-dollar reward in the hands of the Department of Justice.

"Dead or alive, those are the terms." The marshal handed Jack a warrant he had just signed. "You can cash this at any marshal's office, or any bank will discount it for you."

"I don't know as I want it."

"Take it!" the marshal said. "I was a day and a half behind the son of a bitch, and I'm just as happy I never caught up with him."

"Take it," said Dr. Littlejohn.

When the marshal left for Santa Fe, Doc went with him. He returned ten days later with a writ appointing himself executor of Keefe's estate. He had wired the widow from

Santa Fe and had received her reply: PLEASE LIQUIDATE STOP I AM COMING STOP THANK YOU.

"Doesn't tell you much," Jack said.

"She kept a man like Keefe at arm's length all those years. 'Please' and 'thank you' have a different meaning sometimes. We may be in for some interesting times," Doc said thoughtfully.

"Maybe you are. As soon as I get what's coming to me, I'm leaving."

"You can't get it until the estate is closed. Besides, I need your help. How can I liquidate by myself? You're an officer of the court now, Jack. You'll get a hundred a month until we're both dismissed."

Jack began selling horses while Zwicky broke the pintos to harness. Winter fell on them, suddenly and hard, and people stopped passing through Spade Rock. There were no more buyers for horses. Jack sent some to Santa Fe and Albuquerque, to be sold for whatever they would bring. It was cheaper than feeding them.

In less than a month, Zwicky left for Chicago with the pintos and a five-hundred-dollar bonus from the estate. Fowler, the bookkeeper, quit his job, drew his pay, and rode toward warmer winter weather. Jack moved his things out of the house when Mrs. Pepper resigned as housekeeper. He moved into the office, where he practiced the violin long hours every day to keep from going crazy in the dead, empty town. He ate with Chauncey and Doc.

There had been $6,195.50 in cash in the safe when Keefe died. By February 1 there was over $19,000, every dollar of it accountable by vouchers or ledger entries. As of that date, Doc calculated the money that was due Jack as follows:

Share on pinto deal	$1,780.00
Commission on other deals	1,315.00
Back wages to date	585.00
Stud fees by Tom Monk	2,100.00
TOTAL	$5,780.00

"I wonder if my old man ever had that much in cash," Jack mused.

"You see now that you had a good friend in Keefe."

"If I get it."

"You'll get it. The widow won't get a cent until the debts are paid and an accounting made to the court."

"What if she doesn't want to pay me?"

"I'm the executor, Jack. In the unlikely event she contests any item, I'm sure I can prove it to the satisfaction of the court. You are a well-to-do young man."

"That's how money is made, isn't it?"

Doc nodded. "It's a talent, and you have it. I hope it makes you happier than it made Keefe. Did you ever think of him as a happy man?"

"I never did."

"I think he was ready to die a long time ago. I can't feel sorry for him if he got his wish at last. Don't try to understand the human heart, Jack! It's a most curious organ."

A rider came that day from Post Seven to say that the widow was nearing Spade Rock, traveling with a cavalry escort. She had waited for it in Reno, and in Phoenix had bought a house wagon and four horses, and had hired a driver and a wrangler.

"Lieutenant says tell you she has a maid with her. Captain's compliments, and please have quarters ready for her and a fire going," the orderly said.

There was no place for her but Keefe's house. They got a fire going in it and had it reasonably warm, but they had not started to clean it when the procession came jingling into town at a trot. Dr. Littlejohn and Jack went to meet it in front of Chauncey's place.

The woman who descended from the house wagon had a full, matronly figure under a sealskin coat. She looked about in bewilderment, as though thinking that after such a long journey, its end should have shown her more than the dying town of Spade Rock. When she turned her face to Jack, with a puzzled frown on it, he knew why Keefe had lived his lonely, money-making life as he lived it.

She is too beautiful to be real, he thought. A dream that never did come true. . . .

Jet black hair over a high forehead, smoky blue gray eyes, a full mouth held severely in a straight line yet trembling to fulfill something else. He had never seen such white cheeks. The cold had brought spots of color to them that made her forehead look whiter still.

Doc introduced himself and then Jack. The woman gave them both a tiny hand to shake. "It is so good of you to stay on duty here," she said. "I won't pretend to sorrow. One could not help missing Keefe, yet we had been strangers for years."

(A stranger who sent her six thousand dollars a year!)

"He was a cold, self-centered man who thought only of making money," she went on.

(A man who gave a beaten-up kid a home, a fine violin, and a chance to learn how to make money.)

A plump, middle-aged maid emerged reluctantly from the house wagon and stood shivering in terror. Jack and Doc shouldered a mountain of luggage and led the two women up to Keefe's house.

"It is a pigpen," Mrs. Keithly said.

"This town was never more than a work camp, madam," said Doc.

The blue gray eyes smoked. "I'm no stranger to hardship, but filth is something else."

"The housekeeper quit. I did not feel I could justify hiring another one, even if I could find one."

Mrs. Keithly looked at Jack. "You lived here?"

How had she figured that out? He said, "I did. I bunk in the office now."

She turned her back on him and faced Doc. "Where are we to eat?"

"Why, I figured you would cook here—your maid, I mean—the stove draws and heats well—"

"We must care for ourselves? There is no hotel or restaurant?"

Doc drew a long, careful breath. "No madam. I can bring you up something hot from our kitchen, but it will be warmed-over venison and beans, if the beans are done. You will be better suited to cook your own, after this."

Jack tiptoed out, leaving Doc to face it alone. He had never been treated like a servant before. He was not sure he cared for it.

A cattleman had brought Chauncey some fresh eggs this morning, from his wife's flock. Chauncey made fresh biscuits while Doc scrambled eggs. Chauncey also produced a jar of honey and some raisins.

"You serve the lady, Chauncey," said Doc. "I would like to have your opinion."

When Chauncey had gone up the hill with the food, Jack said, "What do you make of her?"

"A bitch," Doc said. "Who but a bitch would stay married to a man all those years, extort all that money from him, and not even let him use his own name? Notice how she speaks of him? She always calls him 'Keefe,' not by his real name."

"It could have been a hell of a life for her, too."

"Jack, a woman like her could keep a man on a chain a thousand miles long. Such women want slaves, not men. With a woman like her, it's war eternal, and total victory or abject surrender. Keefe died, I'll bet, not realizing that he had surrendered."

Jack said, "But you still have to feel sort of sorry for her."

"She's a bitch, Jack. You can't bait her into drawing first, like Rogers. But don't get any ideas! She'll eat you alive and spit you out."

"Ideas? What the hell you talking about?"

They almost quarreled.

Mrs. Keithly's brother, Mr. Blanchard, a San Francisco bank accountant, rode into Spade Rock the next day to assist in auditing the estate. He was old and frail, and the long ride from Albuquerque, and a cold overnight camp, had exhausted him. Yet his sister demanded that they start work on clearing up the estate that same day.

Jack remained in Chauncey's place as much as he could, but again and again he had to be called in to supply details. Again and again he heard Doc say, so politely as to be insulting if you knew him, "There you are, madam. I know you mean no reproach, and I realize that this is painful for you. But as you see, the books are meticulously detailed and accurate."

"I can't understand why the buildings have no value," the woman said. "They made Keefe ten to twenty thousand dollars a year."

"I beg your pardon, madam. Keefe's knowledge of

horses made that money, and it died with him. Jack can testify to what the buildings are worth."

She looked at Jack coldly. He said, "There'll be a few hundred dollars in the lumber from the roof, but that's all."

"Something is wrong when a going concern leaves no more than that behind," she said. "Why, he said he owned the whole town. He said he *was* the town!"

"He was. He is dead and it's dead, madam."

She walked out of the office. Her brother wrung his hands. "You can't reason with her. She was that way even as a child."

"You don't reason with facts," Doc said. "You accept them. Let her have a tantrum in court and see where it gets her."

"I can't afford any more time here and I don't want a scene when I leave. Is there a man who can escort me back to Albuquerque without her knowing I'm leaving?"

"I can find you a man," said Jack. "When?"

"As early tomorrow as possible. God how I dread it! But you can't reason with Yvonne." The old man looked a long time at Jack. "Watch your step. She hates you!"

"Why should she hate me?"

"I don't know, but she does."

When Blanchard had gone to his cold room at Chauncey's place, Jack repeated the question to Doc. "Why should she hate me?"

"Two excellent reasons, Jack. One, you're an independent whelp, you're not servile enough. Two, the money the estate owes you. We can expect trouble on that score. Remember, the money Keefe has been sending her comes to a sudden stop now. Do you think she'll let you get away with nearly six thousand dollars, if she can stop you?"

"Can she stop me?"

"Not if you gut it out and leave it to the court. Don't compromise with her, Jack, whatever you do! She's a bitch, and there's no compromise with a bitch. There is nothing but total victory or unconditional surrender."

Jack could see it that way when he sat talking with Doc or the woman's brother, but when the woman was present, she was like a drink of whisky on an empty stomach. A man saw the same things, but the different lights and shadows gave them different meanings.

He got a rider he trusted, and saw him and Mr. Blanchard off toward Albuquerque at daybreak. Doc came to the office for the books and took them up to the house. Jack worked at sorting, repairing, and tying harness that had been sold to a rancher. He saw neither Doc nor Yvonne Keithly all day.

When night came, he ate supper with Chauncey and Doc. It was so quiet a meal that Jack wondered if Doc had not lost a battle or two of wills with the woman that day. After supper he returned to the office, built up the fire in the stove, lighted a lamp, and got out the violin.

He had tried several times to get back into a routine of regular practice, but always Keefe seemed to get between him and the music. Tonight, somehow, he was able to play for the first time. He tightened the bow and ran a few scales, rising in key until the music was a swift light twitter that was like a trained bird holding its breath.

The door opened and let in a blast of winter air. Mrs. Keithly came in, smiling a rather timid smile at him. Her eyes dropped. Her face, half shadowed and half lighted by the lamp on the shelf behind Jack, was so beautiful it was like being stabbed to see it. The cold was filling the room, but it was not the cold that numbed him. This was a sensation he had never felt before.

"Why don't you shut the door?" he choked.

She closed it behind her. "I wanted to talk to you, Mr. Neely, but I don't want to interrupt you. You play well."

"Only scales." He still choked his words.

She came a few steps closer. "But your phrasing and articulation are perfect! What can you play?"

"A few tunes. . . . Not many. . . ."

"For instance?"

"Well, 'Lorena.' "

"Oh, I know that one! Play it, will you?"

The first note gave him his self-confidence, so he was able to play for himself and not for her. Suddenly she came toward him. They were on the same side of the desk, its length apart. Something in Jack kept warning him,

Don't surrender—don't give anything away—she knows what she's doing and you don't. . . . !

He lowered the violin. She cocked her head and studied him smilingly.

"What did you want to see me about, Mrs. Keithly?"

She ignored his question. "What a beautiful instrument! It's not an Amati, is it? Keefe had one."

"I don't know what its name is, but it was his."

"But why isn't it on the inventory?" she cried.

"Why, he gave it to me. It's mine."

She smiled. "Oh really! You don't imagine I would let you get away with that, do you?"

"Get away with what?"

"Why, taking my husband's violin! You do have nerve, don't you? That, on top of that absurd claim for pay. That's what I wanted to talk to you about, Mr. Neely. I am willing to concede a little—I'll go as high as six or eight hundred dollars—but six thousand, and now Keefe's violin! You must think I'm terribly green."

He put the violin down on the desk. That same warning inner voice kept saying the same thing, and he made himself remember that however beautiful it was, her face was just a human being's face.

"Let's let the court decide," he said.

"Oh really. Do you think I'll let a territorial court decide anything? Mr. Neely, I'll appeal any grant they make to you all the way to the United States Supreme Court, if necessary. Oh, to sponge off my husband for so long, and then when he's gone to think you can conspire to cheat me—oh, detestable!"

He said, "I killed the son of a bitch who murdered Nevil—remember? He was my friend! Do you think there's a person in the Territory who won't testify for me? *I'm* the one who made money for him—*you* bled him like veal. Take it to the Supreme Court, who gives a damn? I'll fight you and beat you and outlive you, because you won't spend a cent of his money until I'm paid."

She snatched up the violin and brought it down across the edge of the desk with both hands. It splintered as Jack reached for her too late. She struck at him with the broken neck of the instrument. His lip stung, and he tasted his own blood.

He unbuckled his gun belt and dropped it under the desk, lest he kill her in cold blood. She misunderstood and screamed and tried to run. Something exploded in him, and he caught her by the collar of her dress and jerked her back. He heard the cloth rip.

She turned and swung the neck of the violin again. Jack slapped her as she struck. He brought the same hand back across her face in a backhand slap. She moaned and fell to her knees. He hauled her to her feet, and she fell against him, supporting herself by her grip on his sleeves.

"Oh no no!" she whimpered. "Oh please, no. No no no no no!"

Without thinking, he put his arms around her and squeezed her face up to his. She kept moaning, "No no no no no," but her lips parted and the word became a panting animal squeal as she kissed him back. And he thought, Poor Nevil! If he had only slapped her a couple of times....

One part of him craved her as he had never craved anything in his life, but another part kept warning him that he could not cope with her, that victory tonight meant unconditional surrender tomorrow. He tore his face away from her and pushed her backward. She fell across the bunk, with her arm across her eyes. In a moment he caught his breath.

"How much was that violin worth?"

"Keefe paid, I think, fifteen hundred for it. I must have been mad, mad! It's worth twice that," she said. She began crying, lying there with her feet on the floor and her arm still across her eyes.

"I'll take fifteen hundred for it, Mrs. Keithly. That makes seventy-two hundred and eighty dollars you owe me."

"What?"

She sat up, white faced and stunned. He said, "If it was five or ten dollars you owed me, maybe we could settle it your way. But you keep that figure in mind, seventy-two hundred and eighty dollars. Every day I go on working here, you owe me another day's pay. It's in the safe, any time I take a notion I'm tired of fooling around with you —and you just keep that in mind, too!"

She walked swiftly to the door and opened it. "Don't think this ends it, you filthy son of a bitch! Nobody ever yet robbed me and got away with it."

"What in the world did you say to her?" Dr. Littlejohn asked.

"We had it out. She lost the argument."

"No question about that, Jack. She ran up the white flag on every point."

Mrs. Keithly had already left Spade Rock in her house wagon, escorted by a squadron of cavalry that would see her all the way to Phoenix. She had signed the inventory of the estate, the list of bills, and the final accounting Doc would submit to the court.

And I guess maybe I'll never know what I missed, Jack thought. . . . The most beautiful woman he had ever known had been his for the taking, and he had not taken her. What was really the difference between victory and defeat—really? I will never know now.

But the important thing now was the money that had piled up here in liquidating the estate. Here it lay, daring any four-bit gang of trouble makers to help themselves to it. No use asking for a cavalry escort for themselves! Troops were for important people like Mrs. Keithly. Their best bet was to make a run for it, before it could occur to anyone to try to take it away from them.

The next day at daybreak, Jack and Doc set out for Santa Fe. They carried the cash from the safe, now risen to more than twenty-five thousand dollars, in saddle bags. They rode hard, made a brief cold camp near morning of the following day to let their horses graze, and by evening were in Santa Fe. Doc's horse was ready to drop. Tom Monk was still fresh.

It took less than an hour to close the legal formalities. Jack put a draft for $7,280 in a waterproof envelope in the pocket of the inner of his two shirts and warned himself to forget he had it.

They remained in Santa Fe until April, Jack living penuriously on his pocket money to keep the draft intact. They started north to Pueblo, Colorado, where Doc wanted to visit a friend before going east. They were a silent pair of traveling companions. Not merely hours, but whole days passed without a word between them.

Riding into Pueblo, Doc said, "Well kid, now what'll you do?"

"Trap myself some wild mares eventually."

"Still going to get rich raising mules?"

"Someday."

"Tell me something, will you?"

"Sure, what?"

"What did you really say to Yvonne Keithly?" Jack did not answer. Doc went on, "All right, but I think maybe you could've tamed her."

"She's twice my age."

"And never met your equal yet. Well, here's where we part, I suppose. Jack, you're a mean little son of a bitch, but I'm going to miss you."

They clasped hands. "I'll miss you too, Doc," Jack said.

Chapter Seven

Tom Monk fought stubbornly against the wind blowing out of a sky that had been scourged clean of clouds. The five men behind Jack had to fight their horses too; but at least he broke the wind for them. They were all in, all of them. And even with luck, they had a four-hour ride ahead of them.

"Neely!"

Jack ignored the shrill shout. It was that man Ollie Shade, the one they called Shady. In a minute, Shady kicked his horse up abreast of Tom Monk.

"This is too much for me, Neely. I'm going to spend the night at Green's. I need a drink and a change of cooking."

"You are like hell." Jack whirled Tom Monk and touched him with his heels. The stud piled into Shady's horse and knocked it sprawling. Shady screamed and rolled out of the saddle, but his horse kept its feet. Shady got up just as Jack tucked his hand under his other arm to pull off his mitten.

Jack pulled his gun and pointed it at Shady and said, "I won't have any trouble out of you. Nobody stops at Green's trap—nobody! Now you ride, boy."

He did not wait to see that Shady obeyed. He turned Tom Monk and rode on, bucking snowdrifts as high as the horse's belly and never for a second escaping the paralyzing keenness of that north wind.

This was his second Wyoming winter. He was a little heavier. He wore a mustache that had come in dark and heavy. He would be twenty-one in July. He had reached an age where, in his wisdom, he knew he had much to learn.

He had been a year and a half on Shipley and Carracker's O Bar O, drawing a hundred a month because he was the man who had killed Dave Rogers. The O Bar O ran five thousand head of cattle and thirty thousand sheep. Any outfit claiming that much land had neighbor trouble, but less of it if their foremen were men of reputation.

In haying and roundup, Shipley and Carracker kept as many as one hundred and fifty hands, in the winter never less than forty. All drew at least sixty a month. They were worth it.

In the winter the crew was divided into two gangs. One of them was run by foreman Elmer Stockdale. Jack Neely was the second winter foreman.

They had gone today to see how the storm had used some crossbred Hereford and Shorthorn bulls that had been winter pastured in a canyon. The bulls had come through fine, but if Jack knew Wyoming weather, another and worse storm was on its way.

He had expected a little trouble from Shady or somebody. Over on the old Oregon Trail, a fellow by the name of Green kept a stage station and store. He had a daughter about thirty, with the mind of a ten-year-old child. Jack had stopped pitying her, because her life seemed to suit her.

But Shady disgusted him, and he knew the O Bar O rules. Ed Clark, the general foreman, held that if a man froze to death, somebody had been a fool. Either it was the man himself, or the man who gave him his orders.

Within an hour heavy black clouds had rolled down out of the mountains. It was still early afternoon, but a lantern would have come in handy. Shady was the fool who had broken theirs this morning.

One of the boys rode up beside Jack and yelled, "I don't see Shady. He must have just dropped back and tailed off some'rs, Jack."

Jack pulled up and looked back. He studied the storm ahead. "Well, it's him for it," he decided. "He's not risking ourselves over. Let's ride!"

Sleet hit them soon, and then snow. They let the horses guide themselves home. There were lanterns hanging everywhere, and plenty of men to take over their horses. All they had to do was roll out of the saddle and go get warm and fill up on hot food.

The O Bar O was really a town—bigger than many a town Jack Neely had seen. Most of the bunkhouse was closed for the winter, but the part still in use held forty men without crowding. Ed Clark broke out a bottle of whisky to warm everybody before they sat down to stew, hot light bread, hot stewed tomatoes, and hot dried-apple pie.

"Ed, I hate it about losing Shady," Jack said. "He couldn't've made it to Green's before she hit. He's out there in it somewhere."

"I hate it, too," Ed said mildly. He was a wiry little gray-haired man, quiet of voice and manner, but as tough as he had to be. "But a man who trains to be a fool is bound to catch the queen of spades sooner or later."

"You ought to move that fellow Green out. Burn his place down, if that's what it takes."

Ed smiled. "He's a friend of Caretaker. They have a lot in common. You don't need to tell Caretaker I said that, Jack."

Ed went into his private quarters at the far end of the bunkhouse building, where he had an office and a living suite, including his private dining room. It was the closest Jack had ever seen him come to criticizing their boss.

"Caretaker" was the men's contemptuous nickname for August Carracker, junior partner in the O Bar O. Shipley lived in New York and came out once a year. Carracker, an Englishman, had not been farther from the ranch than Cheyenne in ten years. Jack had never seen him more than three or four times, but he had heard about his taste for girls who were still children.

"Give us some music, Jack!" somebody said when he went into the big common room in the end of the bunkhouse.

"Not tonight. I'm too tired."

He sat down in a chair beside one of the big stoves and warmed his feet and asked himself questions. He had never really liked it here, but a hundred a month was more than he could make anywhere else. Days and weeks and months had dribbled away, and he had stopped dreaming of a mule ranch.

My luck died with Nevil Keefe, he thought, and I don't know how to make my own luck. . . .

He had seventy-two hundred and eighty dollars in the bank in Pueblo. He had a lot of money coming here, because he had rarely drawn his pay, and Tom Monk had serviced some O Bar O mares. He had a thousand in the bank in Cheyenne, where he had cashed the warrant for the reward for killing Dave Rogers.

And all of it together was still chicken-feed. Those big sums of money Keefe had made were not made by working for somebody else and living in somebody's sock-stinking bunkhouse.

The other foreman came up behind him and said, "Why don't you play the boys some music? You're a pure, no good, worthless hound dog if you don't."

Jack grinned at him. Elmer Stockdale was the strangest specimen of a hired gunman he had ever seen. About twenty-eight, from a good Ohio family, had run away from home at twelve. No trouble, Elmer said—had done well in school and was due to take his place someday in a money-making tannery his father owned. He just decided he wanted to be a cowboy and see Mexico and grizzly bears and the redwood trees, that was all.

He had seen them and he had never regretted leaving home. Big, round-shouldered but powerful, loud and pushy yet at the same time easy-going, Elmer reminded Jack of a big lolloping hound dog. But Elmer was the one man Jack was sure was absolutely without fear.

Life was simple for Elmer Stockdale. Whatever happened, he figured he could probably take care of it. If it turned out he couldn't, he'd likely live through it.

"All right, bring me my harmonica," Jack said.

"You are really a stinking-lazy bastard," said Elmer. He raised his voice to his usual roar. "Bring Mr. Neely his harmonica. Mr. Neely is going to favor the animals with a tune. Everybody kindly kneel down and lick Mr. Neely's hand."

Somebody brought the harmonica. The card games stopped, but they were only pinochle, pitch, and cribbage since gambling as well as liquor was forbidden here. It was a well-run place, the O Bar O, and there were some rules worth remembering if a man ever got a place of his own.

He got the feel of the instrument, running trills and groping for chords that would loosen him up inside. The first tune that always came to mind was "Lorena," and then "Seventh Regiment Bluejackets." He played them, and then some mazurkas and minuets he had learned from Keefe's violin scores.

He knew that music eased some of the winter strain in the men, and made it possible for them to stand each other —and themselves—a little longer.

"Do you know any church music?" somebody said. "How about 'Jesus In My Want I Trust Thee'?"

"If you can whistle it, I can play it."

"I can't whistle worth a damn, but I can sing it."

Jack caught the simple old hymn quickly and began playing it. The man who put his face in his hands and cried was not the one who had asked for the tune. No one laughed.

He played "Turkey in the Straw" and "Irish Washerwoman," and then while Elmer tunelessly sang the words, he played the air for:

> Oh granny, oh granny, me toes are so sore,
> From dancin' over your sandy floor,
> I'll dance ye one jig,
> Then I'll dance no more,
> For I'm goin' home in the marnin'.

He remembered Grandpa Gates on the trombone and himself on the cornet. He remembered the music he had almost learned to play on the violin that bitch had smashed, and he thought, *by God I can't take any more . . .*

He put the harmonica away and walked to Ed Clark's door and knocked. He went in and closed the door behind him. Ed was reading by the light of two enormous coal-oil lamps, with his feet up on a cushioned stool. Ed had comfort here. But comfort was one of the things that could bind you for life as another man's man.

"Ed, how much have I got coming?"

"Why, I would have to look it up."

"I wish you would. Look up what I've got coming for stud service, too."

Ed put his book down and took his spectacles off and held them in his hand. "Why?"

"I'm leaving as soon as this storm ends."

Ed shook his head. "You know the rules."

Shipley and Carracker paid their winter help on May 15, no sooner. There was no other way to hold men in a Wyoming winter.

"I know. But just for the hell of it, let's find out what I've got coming."

Ed went to the paybooks, which showed that Jack would have one thousand three hundred and forty coming at the end of the year, only a few days away. The stud-books disclosed that Tom Monk had stood to twenty mares, at one hundred each.

"A total of thirty-three forty. By May it will be more than four thousand, Jack. Your horse makes more than you do."

"He's worth more. How much has Elmer got coming?"

"If you can talk Caretaker out of your money, I wish you luck, Jack. But you let Elmer alone! How can I spare both of you?"

Jack said nothing. Ed opened the paybook again with a sigh. Elmer had one thousand one hundred and fifty coming.

"Thanks, Ed. I'll tell Caretaker you said no, if it comes to that. But I'll still bet I go and I'll bet I take my money with me."

He went out and motioned to Elmer to follow him into the dining room. They sat down facing each other across one of the long plank tables.

"Elmer, I'm quitting when this storm lets up."

"You won't get your money," Elmer said.

"I'll get it."

Elmer scowled: "What's got into you?"

"This: someday I'm going to have me some grass and

some brood mares and some good Spanish jacks, and raise mules. The longer I put it off, the harder it'll be. I just decided now is the time.

"Mules. I wouldn't give room in the hoglot to a mule. Listen, once I figured I'd spend a year catching me some wild mares in Utah. I have wasted that year, so now I'll have to buy them. You can buy good chunky wild mares for fifty dollars within a day's ride of here. Good ones!"

"Your jack costs you five hundred. Say you have got fifty mares and a jack, you're in for three thousand dollars right there. And you have got three or four years to scrounge a living any way you can, but then you start collecting."

A tough, nimble little mule from a native mare was worth one hundred and fifty at three years. And before three or four years had passed, they should have been able to acquire some big draft mares, past their best working years but still able to produce big mules worth up to two hundred and fifty.

"I see, I see!" Elmer suddenly caught fire. "Listen, I know a spread in the Nebraska sandhills that's just perfect for that. Must be five hundred acres of the best bluestem hay you ever seen, and you've got a lake or a pond never more than a mile away. And you talk about summer range! This is what the Sioux call the Ghost Country—"

His face fell. "It would take better than ten thousand to swing it, and where are we going to get that kind of money? By God, the poor get poorer while the rich get richer! You and me'll be working for somebody all the rest of our natural lives."

"I could raise close to ten thousand," Jack said cautiously.

"You're funnin' me!"

"I'm not."

"I never knowed anybody had that much before."

"Elmer, I've got enough to swing it somewhere. Maybe not the property you're talking about, but a place where we can raise us a crop of mules every year."

"And I be ten percent the owner." Elmer shook his shaggy head. "Not me! If I's bound to work for somebody else, it won't be that kind of a proposition, with the bank gettin' more interest that I do."

Elmer hated banks. Get him on that subject and you could forget everything else. The discussion got nowhere.

But as Jack was getting ready for bed, Elmer threw him a sign to follow him. They returned to the big common room, which was empty now. Only one lamp burned low, and the fires in the stoves had been banked for the night. Elmer made sure they were alone in the big shadowy room.

"You never knowed Buster Pierce, did you? He quit before you came here. Listen!" Elmer put both hands on Jack's shoulders. "I seen him in Laramie last fall. There's a little old country bank in Nebraska, up there near the South Dakota line, that Buster says is purely a cakewalk. Five would be better, but four men can waltz in there and take it without firing a shot. And there's never less than ten thousand in the safe!"

"That's no good, Elmer," Jack said.

"Jack, there's your mule ranch, free for the takin'."

"You must be crazy! Stick up a country bank, and use the money to buy property right next door?"

"It ain't right next door. I want out of here as bad as you do, Jack, but by God I'm not cutting into any proposition where I do all the work and the bank gets all the money. At least promise you'll talk to Buster."

"Let's think it over a few days. There's plenty of time to hit Caretaker up if we decide."

I wish I had never mentioned it to this fool, Jack thought. . . . And yet Buster Pierce was nobody's fool, if what Jack had heard about him was true. You heard a lot about Buster. He was tough and smart and had no fear of any man on earth, and oh how fast he was with a gun!

He vividly remembered Yvonne Keithly. There was a wealthy woman, now, and not likely to stay single long. It would be a day-to-day fight to stay a man, married to her. You could end up tethered on a long chain, like Keefe, if you lost the battle. But if somebody owned your soul, why was Shipley and Carracker any better than Yvonne Keithly?

What was wrong with marrying a rich woman? Somebody was going to marry her.

The wind died down a little, and the snow began. In the morning they found Shady's horse trying to get into the corral. Jack took four men and backtracked him through the storm. They found Shady's body less than three miles from the place.

Apparently the cowboy had changed his mind about Green's and had tried to catch up with them last night. Why he got off his horse, how the horse got away—the snow hid all the answers to those questions. But Shady would cause no more problems to anybody's range boss.

They hacked a grave in the frozen soil of the O Bar O burial ground, where twenty other uniform headstones already stood. Shipley and Carracker took good care of their men, even to furnishing them with carved grave markers. And there I go, too, in a few more years, and who will care? If this is all there is to life, why to hell with it . . .

"Old Caretaker never heard about Lincoln turning the slaves loose," Elmer grumbled, as they fought the blizzard back to the bunkhouse.

Jack said, "Where's this Buster Pierce, and how do you find him?"

Elmer clutched him by the arm. "You mean it?"

"It's going to let up today. I'd like to leave when it does. If we try, we can be in Cheyenne in three days. We've been tethered here too long, Elmer."

As they mounted the porch of the Big House, Jack whispered, "Let me handle this, Elmer. You talk too much."

Elmer nodded. "I know I got a big mouth."

"It's not the worst fault in the world, but this Britisher can out-talk both of us. That's not the way to get at him."

"What is the way?"

"I don't know, but I'll find it. I've got a streak going, Elmer. I don't do anything wrong when I feel the way I feel now."

The fat, breathless manservant whose nickname in the bunkhouse was "Doughface" answered the door. "If you have difficulties, discuss them with Mr. Clark," he said, and tried to close the door. "You know the rules."

Jack put his foot against the door and slammed it back. "My rules say that Mr. Carracker has got three minutes to come out here and discuss, or he'll have his ass full of .45 bullets. Call him now!"

They pushed into the house. Doughface tottered away. Jack had heard of the forty-by-forty living room with its three fireplaces, its ebony piano, and the bearskins that were used to protect fine Oriental rugs. It was all true.

The junior partner came in wearing a green woolen robe. He was a slim man with carefully brushed gray hair and a strange pink flush in his skin. His flinty black eyes had a lizard look in that bony face.

"I suppose you want to quit, men," he said. "We pay in May. You knew the terms when you engaged to stay through the winter."

Jack said quietly, "Guess again, and first let's settle one thing right now. You've got a little gun in the pocket of that robe. Get that hand out where I can see it—empty!—because I'll put two stovepipe holes through you with a .45 before you can draw."

"Threats are no good, my man. That has been tried."

Jack said nothing. In a moment, Mr. Carracker took his hand out of his pocket.

"Usually I live up to any deal I make," Jack said, "but you've had your money's worth out of us. Pay off peaceably, and we go peaceably."

"You ask me to break my own rules. How am I to hold men through the winter, if I do?"

"You'll never hold anybody like us, after we've had enough. You can always find men who'll stay."

"If I refuse?"

"I was coming to that. Let us go, and you lose two men. Refuse, and we go back to the bunkhouse and take the whole crew with us. Then you either pay everybody off, or we burn this house down with you in it," Jack said.

"Today we buried one of your men, and you couldn't get your ass down there to see him spaded under. That's what broke it for me. A one-sided contract is no better than the man enforcing it. You talk it over with Ed Clark, and ask him whether those others will follow me or not."

Carracker pulled at his long lower lip. He nodded. "Very well, upon your word that you won't take anyone else with you, you may tell Ed I said to pay you off."

"We'll give that word."

"Then I am persuaded." A glint of amusement came into the lizard eyes. "You're the chap who owns the black stallion, aren't you? How much do you want for him?"

"He's not for sale. Thank you. We won't bother you any longer."

Jack turned to go. Carracker said, "Another thing, my boy. Ed tells me that in his opinion, you can draw a gun faster than any man alive."

"I wish I could. That's not true."

"Ed thinks so. I've been fair with you. In return, show me how fast you can draw your gun."

Jack shook his head. "When you draw, you shoot. It's all one motion. I'm not a circus performer."

"I should still like to see your fast draw. Why shouldn't I? I'm paying for it."

"You are at that," said Jack.

On the wall behind Caretaker hung a shield-shaped plaque of varnished oak, on it a gilt battle-ax crossed by a blue flower. Jack twisted his body slightly, slapped the gun out into his palm, thumbed back the hammer, and squeezed off a single shot.

The plaque jumped from the wall and crashed in pieces. Carracker had winced from the roar of the gun, but he had not jumped. He touched the fragmented plaque with his toe.

"Our family arms," he murmured. "I wish my brother, the Earl, could have seen that. I am not a bad judge of men at all. Good day, gentlemen."

Outside, Elmer let out a sound that was neither a giggle nor a groan. "Nobody can shoot that straight from the hip," he said. "Nobody!"

"I know that," said Jack, "but Caretaker doesn't."

"Would you really have burnt him out?"

"It was him or us. When it gets down to that sharp a point, Elmer, you have to mean what you say."

Chapter Eight

Somehow time got away from them, and it was late April before they rode into the sandhills. They passed homestead claims, and smelled hogs. Jack's nerves jangled, and Elmer looked unhappy. "To the south, yes, it's sodbuster country," he said. "North is where we're heading."

It was neither fog nor rain that soaked them as they trotted their horses across the low-rolling hills to the property Elmer fancied. It was owned by a widow, a Mrs. Reynolds, who had gone to Omaha to live with her daughter. There were eleven thousand five hundred and twenty acres, plus a lease on twenty-five thousand six hundred more. Some two hundred and fifty head of cattle went with the place.

"They're not much good," Elmer apologized. He seemed to be arguing with himself, as though the property had not lived up to his recollection of it. "A mule would get hog-fat here, though."

Jack got down and kicked at the loose soil. "Elmer, I can dig this grass out with my heel."

"But can you kick out eighteen sections of it? It's short-grass country to be sure, but I can show you draws where the bluestem grows up to your stirrups, and you can put a sandpoint down twenty feet anywhere and you've got a well."

Someone had told them that the price of the property was twenty-two thousand dollars, and that Mrs. Reynolds wanted her equity of some fourteen thousand dollars in cash. It was a lot of money for a little old four-room house and a barn and a lot of sandhill grass, and yet it kept tugging at Jack begging to be liked.

"The winters must be miserable."

"They are, but you don't buy no coconut palms for two dollars an acre. It can cost you twenty cents an acre just to lease, in a good year, and we have got twenty-five thousand acres under lease for a penny an acre."

"Let's look around some more."

They struck a good wagon road, and in a few miles saw a big house with a bigger barn. On the barn was the sign:

Temporary Home
FIRST METHODIST CHURCH
Rev. Amos C. Brown, Minister
WELCOME

"And the same to you, sir," Elmer said. "This wasn't here when I came through a couple of years ago, but I reckon if we leave them alone, they'll leave us alone."

"Not Methodists," said Jack. "You have got Methodists on your hands if they're in a day's ride."

They rode on, and over the first hill beheld a strange sight. A box wagon drawn by four horses hitched abreast came down the hill at a trot. A small, slight girl whose pale hair flew long in the damp air was driving the team, standing up in the wagon with her skirts billowing.

Behind her, a man and what looked like a woman in bib overalls were swinging scoop-shovels rhythmically. Jack and Elmer reined in until the strange outfit came abreast of them. The girl stopped the team. The man put down his scoop shovel and waved them to the wagon. They rode closer.

"Howdy! Stop and visit. The team needs rest and man needs a friendly word, say I."

Elmer said, "What in the name of God are you doing?"

"In His name, sowing oats."

"How'll you cover them?"

"What the Lord wills to sprout, will sprout. One rain and I'll have fat pasture, and maybe some to thresh."

"What if it don't rain?"

"Then that will be the Lord's will too."

"You must be the Reverend Brown," Elmer said uneasily.

"Right you are. My motherless daughters, Louise and Lillian. Your names, gentlemen?"

"I'm Jack and he's Elmer," Jack put in.

The girl driving the team, Lillian, was a beauty, and no more than eighteen. The other one, helping her father scoop oats, a man could almost call fat. Nice pleasant face, nice brown eyes and hair, but she surely did fill those overalls.

"Looking over the Reynolds property?" Reverend Brown said. "There's no better anywhere."

"We heard about it," Jack said. "Do you suppose it's a firm price?"

"Like a rock, Mrs. Reynolds says. But it has gone unsold for two years, and an offer might be taken. Her agent is a lawyer in Salcomb, five miles east, county seat, thriving town lacking only in churches. I take it you boys are family men?"

"Single as the day we was born," Elmer said.

The preacher's face widened in a sunny smile. He sized Jack and Elmer up with a horse trader's skill.

"You must settle down sometime, say I, and you look like steady young men to me. There's a fortune in this place if you have the will to work."

Elmer would have stayed gossiping forever, but Jack tipped his hat and rode on, and there was nothing for Elmer to do but follow.

"A man with two daughters, you cain't blame him for looking to their prospects," Elmer said.

"I guess not."

"Jack, let's buy that property! I only hope to God somebody don't beat us to it. We'll marry them two girls. I'll take the oldest one and you take Lillian."

"If nobody beats us to them, too."

What would it be like to have that slim, sweet, silent Lillian to come home to, on a wet, lonely day like this one?

"The way to see you don't get beat is get there first," said Elmer.

"I doubt I'll ever marry, Elmer. We have bad luck with women in my family."

"You aim to shoot your way through the rest of your life? They ain't all going to lay down and die like Dave Rogers! Someday one of them will shoot first."

"That's always a possibility."

They rode in silence for a while. Then Elmer said, "Jack, of all the women you ever knowed, who was your favorite and what was she like?"

"She was too old for me, and too pretty, and too rich. I have not had much to do with women, and I haven't missed them."

"One will deadfall you sure, one of these days," Elmer grumbled. "Contrary to what you think, it ain't the man who likes the ladies that gets into trouble with them. It's the woman-haters like you."

They rode past the Ripley National Bank and looked it over surreptitiously. It was Saturday, and the town was full. They attracted no attention. They fed their horses in the public stable while they ate in the hotel, and in another hour were on their way.

"What do you think, Jack?"

"It's not even in the sandhills."

"What's that got to do with it?"

"You said a sandhill bank."

"That's what Buster Pierce called it."

"This is the Niobrara Valley. We start out with a description that's all wrong, and I don't see any reason for it to have all that money in it. I don't see how it's any easier than any other bank to stick up."

"Wait till you talk to Buster, that's all!"

Jack turned in the saddle. "I'll tell you something else, Elmer. I never yet saw a grown man that went by a baby name like 'Buster' or 'Buddy' that was worth a damn at anything."

"Listen, have you suddenly got a conscience?"

"Well, I've never taken a dime from anybody yet that I hadn't earned, and I'm thinking hard."

Elmer raged, "A poor storekeeper, no. But the sons of bitches with money enough to start a bank, there's only two things you can do. Pay them ten percent until they foreclose on you, or take a gun and take it away from them. It don't bother my conscience none!"

They picked up word of Buster in Valentine. They tracked him almost up into the Black Hills, where they heard he was drilling wells in a little town called Wild Rose, in Nebraska. They rode southward two days, and at last picked up the tracks of his shod horse.

"I know them tracks," said Elmer. "He rides a big spotted mare that'll weigh close to ten-fifty, and he shoes her heavy in the toes. But there are two fellers riding with him. I only hope he hasn't already got his gang."

"It won't cost me any sleep if he has."

Late that afternoon they lost the sign. They separated to seek it, and Jack almost lost interest too. Let Elmer have this fool deal, he thought. I don't want to hold up any banks. . . .

"Stop right there and get them hands up," a voice said.

The twin barrels of a shotgun were pointing at him from across a man-high rock. Jack raised his right hand, saying, "If I raise the other one, this stud goes up like a firecracker. You've got the drop. Say what you want done, and I'll do it."

"Just set!"

A big man wearing a tall black hat, and with a mane of curly black hair and a coarse black moustache, stepped out from behind the rock. He carried the shotgun in his big hand like a pistol.

"You been on my tracks for two days. Why?"

"We heard you were drilling wells in Wild Rose."

"Who heard?"

"Elmer Stockdale and I."

"I don't know any Elmer Stockdale."

"He knows you. You're Buster Pierce."

"You're mighty free with names. Where might we run into this Stockdale fellow you mention?"

"Let's just set. He'll find me."

Soon Elmer rode up, slid off his horse, and threw both arms around the big man with the moustache. "Buster, you're harder to trail than a greased snake!" he bellowed. "What the hell is this about you drillin' wells? That's too much like work! Meet my sidekick, Jack Neely."

Pierce grinned an attractive grin and let Elmer pound him on the back. He put his hand out to Jack, saying, "I've heard of you, I bet. You're the kid that killed Dave Rogers, right? I knowed Dave. They say you are some fancy with a gun."

They sat around a fire with Pierce and his two friends and talked it over. Jack was willing to listen, but Pierce had spoiled it a little when he mentioned Dave Rogers. I am getting tired of hearing about that, Jack thought. Everybody knew him personally. And I'll bet there are more people claiming to know me personally. . . .

He was not sure how he felt about Pierce's two friends. Owen Simington was a quiet, shabby, middle-aged man with a look of some deep sickness about him. Somewhere he had a family to provide for before he died, Jack was sure. The Ripley National Bank was his insurance policy.

Marcus Peek was slight and girlish looking, and no more than twenty. Any kid with his smooth pink cheeks and long eyelashes had to be tough, or simply be teased to death.

Pierce used his jackknife to draw diagrams in the dirt. "Owen and I go in the front door, about half a minute apart. Jack and Elmer wait until we're inside, then you come in the other door. It's a corner bank, see, with a door on each—"

"I know. We looked it over," Jack said.

Pierce squinted at him. "Why?"

"Why not?"

Pierce looked down at his diagram again. "Owen will have the shotgun broke in two, under his jacket. When Jack and Elmer, here, are in place, Owen faces the wall and snaps the shotgun together. Now he'll have that done before anybody realizes anything. When he's ready, he turns around with the gun, and I tell them it's a holdup.

"I let go a shot into the ceiling to show we mean business. Owen and Jack and Elmer cover, while I go into the vault. When I come out with the money, Jack or Elmer, whichever can whistle the loudest—"

"I can whistle fit to bust your ears," Elmer said.

"Then you whistle, and Marcus brings the horses to the side door. Now I lock the front door from the inside, and jam the padlock with axle grease and iron filings. It'll jam a lock every time! We all go out the side door.

"Now get this! The side door opens *outward.* Marcus carries a chunk of two-by-four. We prop the door shut with it, and nobody can get out. I let go a couple of shots in case anybody on the street has any ideas, and we head north out of town.

"North, remember, but only to that new sheep-shearing shed in the cottonwoods. We just ride into it and hole up until dark, and then I'll show you how to slide past them sheep camps to the east and not leave a track in ten miles. How's that sound to you?"

"It'll work," young Peek said shrilly.

"I've never seen the bank," said Simington, "but I'll take your judgment, Buster."

Buster and then Elmer looked at Jack. Jack said, "It's almost too good to be true, but I'd like to think it over."

"Take all the time you want!"

"One thing, will you ride that spotted mare of yours?"

"Why not?"

"You might as well leave your calling-card. Anybody would pick that horse out of a herd, anywhere."

Buster nodded soberly. "You're right. Well, I'll tie her in the sheep-shearing shed and borrow somebody's horse for the job. Otherwise, Jack, you got to admit I have got a cat at every rathole."

This Buster carried you along. Just the size of him made you believe. But Jack thought it over for two days, and then Pierce's spotted horse slipped her hobbles and got away. Jack and Elmer went after her, they having the only horses that could run her down.

They caught the mare and started back. Jack waited until they were close to camp, until he was surer in his own mind.

"Elmer, you and Marcus and Owen can do as you please, but I owe it to you to tell you I don't want any part of this bank proposition."

Elmer leaned back on his reins. *"Wha-a-at?"*

"I'll never say anything to anybody. But I won't go along."

"But what about the mule ranch?"

"That's why it took so long to decide. I never gave up anything so hard in my life, but all Buster is fixing to do is get somebody killed."

"But you heard his plan! By God, I guaranteed you! He asked me last night if I was sure of you."

"Oh he did! What did you say?"

"I said I'd count on you to the last trump."

"And then he said that saved him from having it out with me, didn't he? He said he'd take your word, but otherwise he'd have a talk with me. That's what he said, am I right, Elmer?"

"Well yes, but—"

Jack shouted, "Don't you see? That curly headed show-off can't keep his mind on the bank. He wants to be the son of a bitch that killed the son of a bitch that killed Dave Rogers. And his plan—oh hell, what a plan to rob a bank!"

"What's wrong with his plan?"

"He sashays in there and everybody picks his nose while Owen puts a shotgun together. He shoots into the ceiling for no reason except to bait some fool into shooting back. How does he know that sheep-shearing shed is going to be empty long enough for us to hole up there and make off again?

"Suppose it's a hot day—how will Owen look wearing a jacket to hide the shotgun? Suppose it rains and you leave a trail even in grass? Suppose that grove is full of blackbirds that are still spooked after we have gone into the sheep-shearing shed, and are still flying around in circles when the posse rides by? Elmer this fool couldn't plan a Sunday-school picnic!"

Elmer liked and trusted everybody, but he was no fool. He took off his hat and mopped his troubled face with his sleeve. "I don't see why I didn't think of them things, or Peek or Simington."

"Pierce could talk a badger out of his hole, but he has got only one thing on his mind, Elmer. There's a kind of man that can go through life just so far, and then he's got to kill somebody—beat up on somebody—take it out on the world some way—"

In his mind Jack could hear Doc saying, as he knelt beside Dave Rogers's body, "Well, you finally got there, didn't you?" Yes he had, and you never could go back.

"Jack, what the hell are we going to do?" Again Elmer mopped his face. "He won't stand for us pulling out."

"If he tries to stop me, I'll kill him."

"If you pull out, I pull out too."

"All right, but you talk too much. You let me handle this big, windy, curly-headed fellow."

They hazed Pierce's horse back into camp, and Pierce staked her out securely. "You taken your time getting back, Neely," he said.

"We did for sure," Jack said. He got off Tom Monk and slapped the stud on the belly, to move him away.

"What's that supposed to mean?" said Pierce.

"Tell you in a minute. I want Marcus and Owen to hear this too. You boys!"

Peek and Simington got up from where they had been dozing under a tree. "What's up?" old Owen said.

"I'm quitting this bank proposition," Jack said. "Give me a day's start, and I'll never talk. But one thing is sure, I am dealing myself out."

"But why?" young Peek said, almost in a wail.

"Because all Buster is going to do is get somebody killed. Maybe one of us. Maybe some fool working in the bank, or some woman in there doing business. Rob a bank without anybody being shot—that's one thing. But kill somebody the way I think Buster means to do, and they hound us until the State of Nebraska hangs every man!"

Buster Pierce said, "Jack, you went along fine until now. You never had any complaints about anybody getting shot before this."

Pierce had to argue. He had to nerve himself up to the peak where he dared to draw on the man who had killed Dave Rogers. All his life he had been seeking a moment like this one, and now here it came.

"But I thought it over, Buster," Jack said.

Pierce dared a quick look at Elmer. "How about you?"

"Deal me out, too," Elmer said. His voice rose, "And

for God's sake, don't try anything because Jack will kill you if you do!"

"You have got me in the middle," Buster said. "The two of you, two against one. What can I do?"

"You're not in any middle," Jack said. "Take a minute or two and cool off, Pierce. There is no need of any trouble. You go your way and we go ours, and all the luck in the world if you go ahead with the bank."

"What can I do?" Pierce said again.

He stood a little higher than Jack, near the fireplace they had built with soapstone slabs from the creek. Behind Pierce, Jack could see steam rising from the spout of the coffee pot. In a minute you would be able to smell the good smell of coffee all over the—

Pierce started to turn, as though giving up. His body swiveled but the soles of his feet remained firm on the ground, and he went for his gun. Jack let him get his hand on it, suffering one searing pang of fear because the big bluffer moved like a snake.

He slapped his own gun out, hooked the hammer, and shot Pierce in the chest. Pierce's big legs pumped him one step forward, but he was already dead. Blood gushed from his mouth and nose as he pitched forward on his face.

"I told the fool, didn't I?" Elmer bellowed. "But he had to try!"

The four of them sat around the fire until the night was half gone. They had buried Pierce and turned his fine spotted mare loose. They had eaten supper and drunk the pot of coffee, and then another pot.

"Somebody say it," Jack said. "Nobody's going to sleep until everybody gets it out of his system."

"Oh God, I needed that money!" young Marcus Peek moaned.

"Marcus, everybody needs money."

"Not like me. I want to get married."

"How do other people get married? They don't all rob banks."

"They haven't already got the girl knocked up, either. She's a good girl, and there's just her and her mother. They have to take in sewing, and now look!"

"I feel sorry for her, but I'd feel a lot sorrier if Pierce had got you killed, kid."

This Peek kid was another one who would always be in trouble of some kind. Old Man Simington was another problem. It was he who had gone out and shot the antelope that made their supper, he who had cooked it, he who had moved the camp away from the spot where Buster Pierce had died.

"Listen, Jack," Simington said.

"I know what's coming, Owen. You've got a hard-luck story too."

"I've got a year to live, if I'm lucky. I've got a wife and five kids in Minneapolis, living on what I can send them. There must be *some* way to clean out that bank. You figured out what was wrong with Pierce's plan. Now what's the right way to do it?"

Jack looked at Elmer, who looked back with the soft eyes of a kicked dog. Elmer was thinking of that chubby preacher's daughter in her overalls. All that was good, and all that was bad, in his simple nature was taking dead aim at one thing—marrying Louise Brown and settling down on that sandhill mule ranch.

"There's a way, but if you take my plan you take my orders too. And the first one is this, if there's any shooting, I do it. I pack the only loaded gun, and anybody who doesn't like it, now's the time to say so."

"However you cipher it suits me, Jack," Elmer said eagerly.

"Anything you say, Jack," young Marcus Peek murmured; and Owen Simington said, "Deal me in."

"All right then, which one of you, Elmer or Owen, can come closest to looking like a preacher?"

"A what?" Elmer blurted.

"A sky-pilot, a missionary to the sodbusters, a revival shark."

"I would play hell," Elmer said.

"I have been ordained by the Tabernacle Covenant," Owen Simington said. "I have backslid into sin, but nothing can keep me from looking the part. Nothing wipes out God's ordination, they say. I ain't so sure of that however."

"It's good enough." It's almost too good to be true, Jack thought. I'm going over a cliff head first, but the hell with everything, let's rob this bank. . . . "All right, here's how we'll do it. . . ."

Chapter Nine

It was the rain they had waited for, a three-day sod-soaker. The old shed on the flooded creek, on the edge of Ripley, had been somebody's homestead shanty once. Its sod walls would not stand many more hard rains, and its patchwork roof leaked everywhere.

It was light enough to see lamps in a few windows. Jack touched Peek's shoulder. "You'll have a long wait, but better go now," he said.

"What bothers me," said Marcus, "is this empty shotgun. I'm just a hog for butchering, unarmed."

"We can call it off."

"No, I'm just bellyaching, Jack."

Peek hung the shotgun by its trigger guard, to a wire hook on his belt, under his slicker. He slipped out and vanished in the rain. So far as Jack could tell, no other person was afoot in Ripley.

"Now you go, Owen. Let's check the gun."

Owen broke his gun and spun the cylinder to show it was empty. He gathered himself in his slicker and sloshed away after Marcus. Elmer moved up to where he was breathing on Jack's neck.

"Go now, but you're the key man, Elmer," Jack said. "If you let yourself be seen, it's all off."

"I won't be seen." Elmer yawned. He did not seem to have a nerve in his body. "This rain will make Rev'rend Brown's oats. What will a couple of hundred tons of oat hay be worth next winter? God!"

He left the shanty. Jack made a cigarette and smoked it slowly. Here I am, he thought, with ten thousand dollars in the bank, and robbing another one. Why? I can still back out. And if I don't, tomorrow some of us could be dead, the others on the way to the pen. . . .

He was crossing a line he had never crossed before, and he did not understand how he had come here. He was sure of one thing: no man, himself included, could say that it was the last, the one and only, time. Get away with something like this once, and who would want to work for a living again?

Why was he doing it? He could not blame Elmer, whose simple mind and heart had just room for that preacher's daughter, now. It was not money, because he already had that. Not for the dream of a mule ranch.

No. Just to show he could do it. He threw his cigarette away and went out of the shanty. The creek was less than a hundred yards away. In ordinary weather it was not more than three or four feet wide. Now it ran forty feet from bank to bank, and would rise still more before this rain abated.

Last night, while the creek was narrower, they had stretched a rope across it, securing both ends to box elder trees. The rain had shrunk it taut. Jack crossed hand over hand on the rope, his boots no more than a foot above the water.

Four horses that they had stolen up in South Dakota were halter-tied on the other side. One at a time, he slipped their bits and fed them wet oats so they would shut up and stay shut up. He bitted them again and returned to the shanty to wait for Mr. J. A. Tracy, President of the Ripley National Bank, to come to work.

Everything was ready. Marcus waited in the crotch of a tree beside the side door of the bank. In this weather, no one would be looking up in the leaves for a man with a shotgun.

Owen and his empty six-gun were in the storage shed back of the store, next door to the bank. They had pried the staple loose the night before. All Owen had to do was pull off the hasp and go in and stay dry. He was a sick man and he needed it.

Across the street from the bank front was an old frame house, now a harness shop, with five steps up to the door. Under the high porch, the village dogs took shelter. There Elmer now waited with his empty gun, and not a dog barked. Elmer had a way with dogs.

Men appeared on the street—the hostler from the livery stable and the man who swept out the saloon, on their way to work. More and more people appeared, but they did not linger in the downpour. At 8:20 A.M. a plump, strutting man hurried down the street under a black umbrella. Mr. J. A. Tracy, a Kentuckian who had come here a year ago, was on his way to open the bank.

Jack timed it to meet him at the door. As Tracy bowed his head under his umbrella to search for the right key on his ring, Jack tied on his mask. The others all had the same kind of masks, cut from a faded gray dress pulled off a Dakota clothesline weeks ago. All wore the same black slickers and the same punched-in black hats. Witnesses were going to have trouble testifying to anything.

The banker found the right key and opened the big padlock. Jack pushed the muzzle of his gun into Tracy's back. "This is a .45. You're being held up," he said softly.

"Oh my God!" the banker said.

"Shut up!" Jack prodded him with the gun. "Go inside. Take the padlock with you. Do as you're told, and nobody will get hurt. It's up to you."

The banker lurched into the bank. Jack followed him, took the padlock from him, and dropped it into the pocket of his slicker.

"Unlock the other door. Don't pay any attention to anybody else who comes in! There's a woman clerk due next. What's her name?"

"That's Miss Nichols. You've got the drop. Whatever you say, that goes," the banker quavered.

"You make sure Miss Nichols knows it. You can't always tell how an old maid is going to act up."

Elmer came in the front door. "The woman is coming, Mike. I'll handle her."

Jack saw Marcus slide out of the tree. He heard a thud, a little louder than he expected. It was the rock Marcus had thrown against the side of the shed out back, to notify Owen that it was time.

By the time the banker had the side door open, Owen was ready to slip inside, his empty gun in his hand. Marcus remained on watch outside, the shotgun still hidden under his slicker.

"Polite now, Mike!" Jack called to Elmer, as the woman came in the door and shook out her umbrella.

Elmer stepped behind her and put his arm around her to cover her mouth with his hand. "It's a holdup, miss," he said softly. "Nobody's going to hurt you, but you better behave, you hear?"

She was small and gray haired, one of those smart, capable spinsters who never seem to age past a certain time. She snarled at Elmer, "Nobody had better hurt me! I'll live to see you all hang, you sons of bitches!"

"Now we'll go into the vault, Mr. Tracy," Jack said.

"It takes two to open it. I have only a half of the combination."

"Shit! Open the vault."

Jack herded Tracy ahead of him. While the banker spun the dial, Jack took from his slicker pocket a large square of oilcloth and the two sleeves from the old gray dress that had made their masks. The door of the safe opened silently. Inside, a candle was stuck by its own grease to the stone walls, with a box of matches beside it.

Jack lighted the candle. "Sit down. I won't lock you in if you behave, Mr. Tracy. It's up to you."

Tracy sat down on the stool that belonged in the vault. Jack searched it quickly for a gun and found none. He knelt beside the hardwood box-drawers that held the cash. He wrapped the currency in the oilcloth and stuffed it into one of the sleeves. Gold coin went into the other sleeve.

He did not bother with silver. "All clear, Mike?" he called out.

"All clear!" Elmer replied.

Jack picked up his gun. "Come on, Colonel."

"Colonel?" Tracy quavered.

"Ain't you Kentuckians all colonels? I never heered of no enlisted men from there!"

He deliberately emphasized his Texas drawl as he pushed the banker out of the vault. Elmer said, "They was a gun in his nib's desk, but that's all."

"Lock the front door, Mike."

Elmer took the new padlock from his pocket and locked the front door from the inside. Jack said, "Both of you sit down now, and take off your boots. That goes for you too, Miss Nichols."

When the woman's hand shook too hard for her to remove her shoes, Elmer knelt and helped her. He put her right shoe and one of the man's boots in his pocket.

"That does it, Mike," he said to Jack.

Jack looked at Owen. "Here we go! Tell Mike to cover us with the shotgun." He looked at the banker and Miss Nichols. "Holler whenever you feel lucky. We won't hurt you, Miss Nichols, but if we have to blow Mr. Tracy in two with a shotgun, we will do it."

She snarled at him, "I'll live to see you hang, you Texas riffraff, you Reb scum, you greasers!"

"You're not goin' to make any friends for this bank thataway," Jack drawled to her.

He pitched the two sleeves of money to Owen, who holstered his empty gun and went out. Elmer went next, to throw the two shoes as far as he could throw them. Jack stepped out and pulled the door shut, and Owen locked it from the outside with another new padlock.

A man was staring at them from across the side street. "You've got a customer, Mike," Jack said loudly. Marcus jumped out from behind the tree and aimed the shotgun across the street, screeching, "Don't you move! And don't you make a sound or I blow your goddamned head off!"

The man closed his mouth so hard they heard his teeth click. Jack, Elmer, and Owen walked toward the creek. Marcus followed them, the shotgun as ready in his hands as an unloaded gun could be. Where the brick walk ended, they began running.

Elmer crossed the creek first. Jack swung the two sleeves of money around his head and slung them across to Elmer, who chuckled as he caught them. Jack slapped Owen on the shoulder and Marcus on the bottom.

"Get over there fast! Get those horses untied, but wait for me."

The creek was higher, and he had to double his knees up under him to keep his feet out of the water. He cut the rope and let it trail in the swift current. As he mounted, he saw someone on the far side of the creek run up and snatch up the shotgun that Marcus had dropped where the sidewalk ended. Wait until he tried to fire it!

"It went off like play-acting!" Marcus cried.

"We're not out of it yet," Jack said, "but we will be if we all do our jobs."

Half a mile to the west there was a wooden wagon bridge over the creek, and not a track or rut to show that anyone had been on the road. They walked their horses over the bridge to reduce the noise, kicked them into a run, and headed north.

Another half-mile and they crossed a triangular section of swamp pasture. The sheep-shearing shed that had been so important in Buster Pierce's plans was in sight now. Beside it stood a covered wagon, with a tarp stretched beside it to shelter a little cooking fire. On the wagon sheet was the legend, in red, yellow, and black:

Repent, for the kingdom of heaven is at hand!
GLORY CRUSADE!!!
Reverend John Culligant

Two crowbait horses, already harnessed, were tied nearby. Under the cottonwoods, already saddled, stood Tom Monk.

They dismounted and stripped the saddles and bridles from their stolen horses. One at a time, Elmer whacked them viciously as they ran free. They would not stop running much this side of South Dakota; and in this rain, their tracks would be gone in minutes.

The horses were not out of sight, however, before Jack and Marcus had wrestled the plank cover from an old dug well. They dropped the saddles, bridles, masks, and black hats and slickers down the well, and slid the cover back in place. . . .

The town was in sight by the time Jack saw the five riders coming toward them. They were galloping hard, risking their horses in bad footing and kicking up a storm of mud. He spurred Tom Monk out in front of the old crowbait team and opened his slicker. He sat there waiting with his hand on his hip, near his gun.

"Now hold it!" he shouted stridently. "If there's trouble, I'll start it, and by God I can finish it too!"

Behind him, on the seat of the covered wagon, Owen said clearly, "There is no call to swear. We are not afraid."

The leader of the five riders shouted, "Get your hand away from that gun! I'm a deputy sheriff and—"

This was Jack's moment, to make them or break them. He said furiously, "And where the hell were you last night, when those sons of bitches were abusing these people?" He pointed behind him at Marcus, in a girl's dress, with a sodden bonnet tied over her head. "She's only fifteen years old. They like to ripped the clothes off her. What the hell kind of county do you run?"

"There is no need to swear," Owen said again.

"Who are you?" the deputy demanded.

"The name is Jack Neely."

"What are you doing in—*Jack Neely?* Oh hell, Mr. Neely, we're looking for bank robbers."

"You're not looking very hard, any more than you are for the four renegades that hazed this old man and this kid. If I hadn't come along—"

"Four renegades? Four? How was they dressed?"

Jack told his story. He had stopped last night when he saw the cook-fire next to that sheap-shearing shed back there.

"I saw that fire, too, last night," a member of the posse said. "Miserable night to be out, Reverend."

The preacher and his daughter had given Jack Neely coffee, corn-bread, and some fried rabbit. The four men had stopped a few minutes later, and they had to have a kiss with their cornbread. Jack had got the drop on them, and they lost their passion suddenly when he squeezed one off at them. All he knew was that one was called Mike.

"The way I get it, they was all named Mike. Well, I am sorry to say you didn't hit nobody, Mr. Neely." He tipped his hat to Owen and Marcus. "Sorry you had that trouble, but they wasn't Ripley County boys."

"I'll ride with them a piece, just to make sure we don't run into any more visitors to the county," Jack said.

They camped that night on the prairie, miles south of Ripley. After dark, Elmer could come out of the wagon and stretch his legs, but he had to hide again at daylight. The next day they made another fifteen miles. That night they brought their own lazy, rested horses out of somebody's fenced hayfield. They turned loose the crowbaits that had pulled the wagon, burned the wagon and harness, and divided the loot.

"Don't any of you complain that it's not as much as Buster promised you," Jack said. "It's a lot more than belongs in that little old country bank."

There was eight thousand, three hundred and twenty in the two sleeves, two thousand and eighty for each of them. Owen and Marcus struck eastward together, planning to avoid trials and towns all the way to the Missouri. There they would separate. Jack and Elmer shook hands with them and headed southward together.

It was a hot and humid June tenth when they passed Reverend Brown's place. The oats would make a crop. As far as they could see, strong green stems rippled like an ocean.

"Jack!" Elmer bawled. "That pious old scamp planted half of his crop on our land."

"Our land?"

"It will be soon. With what you got in the bank, and what the two of us is carrying, we got plenty!"

Jack said, "Elmer, we can't turn up any cash money now. Minute we show any of this bank money, they throw us into jail. Every banker, every storekeeper, every lawman in Nebraska will be on the lookout for big spenders now. We've got to swing it on what I can account for from what I've got in banks."

"Jack, I want that land more than anything I ever wanted in the world, but I ain't no bank robber." Elmer pounded the side of his head with his hand. "Why did I do it? Why? We're no better off than we were before we robbed the damn bank!"

"I knew that all along. This is going to take some thinking. I reckon if I wasn't ready to settle down before we robbed that bank, I am now. Another thing, Elmer—I'm going back to my real name. Henry Ely."

"Henry Ely?"

"Henry Ely."

"That name don't mean nothing."

"That's why. I'm going to shave off my moustache too. I would like to feel like my old self again."

They camped that night on the creek near the town of Salcomb. He shaved his face clean, but he still did not feel like Henry Ely.

In the morning they hunted up the sheriff who, since the courthouse was still only a blueprint, ran his office from a room over the bank. "My name is Henry Ely, and this is Elmer Stockdale. We're interested in that Reynolds property."

The sheriff shook hands. "Deal is my name, Omicron Deal. George Weedy is Mrs. Reynolds's lawyer. You go right across the hall and the first door to—"

"You come with us, please. There's a reason."

Deal was a big man, gray haired and gone to fat, but he had the look of a public servant who could be pushed just so far. He went to the lawyer's office with them.

"We know what she's asking and we know she wants cash," Jack said. "Cash is out! We'll give her ten thousand dollars. Seventy-five hundred within sixty days, the balance in a year. Of the seventy-five hundred, we can put up twenty-five hundred now."

Weedy drummed on the desk. "She won't take it."

"If she can make a better deal anywhere else, let her have at it."

"Twenty-five hundred down. Where will you raise the other five thousand within sixty days?"

"I've got it in a bank in Colorado, drawing interest for two years now. More than enough!"

"How do you propose to make a living there, and pay twenty-five hundred more within a year?"

"We're going to raise mules. I know people who can put up the money if I have to write to them. We've got the ten thousand but we're not going in there broke. We'll need money for brood mares and stud jacks.

"I can make money buying and selling horses. You'll want references, if you take our notes for the balance due in a year. The people that know both of us are Shipley and Carracker, that's the O Bar O, in Wyoming."

"I know that outfit," Sheriff Deal put in. "Who is their superintendent now?"

Elmer said, "They haven't got any superintendent. Mr. Carracker is resident manager. The general foreman is Ed Clark. We were both foremen under him."

"I've knowed Ed Clark for thirty years," Deal said, and Jack could have wept with relief. "I'll write to him, Mr. Weedy, if you want."

"Wire him! But there is one more thing," Jack said. "To get the pay we had coming, we had to threaten to burn Carracker out. You may as well find that out from us as from them."

"Would you have done it?"

Jack looked the old man in the eye. "I don't know. I like to think I wouldn't, but I just don't know."

"What do you think, Mr. Weedy?"

"If you're satisfied with these men, Omicron, I will recommend it to the old lady," the lawyer said.

"If Ed Clark is satisfied, I am too."

They signed an agreement to purchase and handed over a dollar to bind the deal. When they left the lawyer's office, Jack told Elmer to meet him down on the street. He stepped into the sheriff's office and closed the door behind him.

"One thing more, sheriff. This is for your ears only, and if it doesn't suit you, we call the whole deal off. When you wire Ed Clark—or the bank in Pueblo, where I've got my money—they're not going to have an idea in the world who Henry Ely is."

"I see. You used another name?"

"Jack Neely. Mean anything to you?"

The sheriff scratched his crotch, studying Jack meanwhile with those crafty office-seeker's eyes of his. "Didn't you—wasn't it Jack Neely who collected the reward from them Mormons for killing Dave Rogers?"

"That's part of the money in the Pueblo bank."

"How are you going to get it out? Jack Neely put it in, Henry Ely takes it out. Seems to me like you got some explaining to do first."

"I'm not the first man to use two names. I don't expect anybody is going to drop dead from surprise. You're not asking them about a wanted man, sheriff. You're investigating the character of a land-buyer who told you the truth. A lot is going to depend on the way you put the questions to them."

The sheriff thought it over with the stubborn slow gravity that seemed to be characteristic of him. When his face suddenly softened, when he stood up with an understanding smile twitching at his hard mouth, Henry knew he had won.

Suddenly he felt like Henry Ely again.

Chapter Ten

Still no break in the heat, yet frost was surely less than a month away. Henry eased his bad leg out of bed and put that foot in a carpet slipper. He slid the other into its boot, and reached for his cane.

It was late September and he had been alone on the place for two weeks. He had put together a string of sixteen horses, for which he figured Remount should pay up to one hundred fifty each. Elmer had taken them to Grand Island to try his luck. He could not go far wrong, since the horses averaged out at a cost of about sixty dollars each.

Henry would have been in Grand Island himself, only the day before he was to leave he had let Screamer back him into a fence and step on his foot. Screamer was the big black Spanish jack that had cost them five hundred dollars, sight unseen, in Omaha. It was bad enough for a grown man to let a horse bang up a foot and ankle for him. But this—well, Screamer hadn't been the only jackass in that little collision.

There were twenty-one wild young mares in the big fenced pasture that were carrying Screamer's colts. Thirteen more stood in the corral, awaiting their turns. They were in the mule business.

As Henry fried his breakfast eggs, someone hailed him from outside. He hobbled to the front door and saw Herman Lozik, a Bohemian homesteader from down on Douglas Creek. Herman did most of the translating for the other Bohunk squatters.

With him was a countryman whom he introduced as Louis Sedlacek. "Louie got damn good idea, Henry. He no talk English so I talk for him."

They had eaten, but they would have a cup of coffee with Henry.

"Louie brick maker, tile burner, in Old Country. Your hill north of house, past creek, all beautiful white pipeclay. Make very fine brick. Louie want make brick."

"Tell him go ahead. Just don't leave any gates open, Herman."

"You no understand. He want start big brickyard, Henry. Buy a press. Make two thousand brick a day!"

"What in tarnation does he want with so many?"

"Sell! No brickyard two hundred mile. Make all nice terra-cotta brick, very classy. He want go partners with you. It take money to buy press. You got hire men, too. Cost money, but my God how you make money!"

"Herman, we can't pay for what we've got."

Herman would not listen. He got out a pencil to show how Louie and four men could press and burn a thousand fine terra-cotta bricks every five hours. They would sell for one cent each. They would cost one-half cent each. After the press was paid for, that cost would decline to a quarter of a cent each.

Henry could figure in his head. "Fine, that's a dollar an hour, but who buys all the bricks?"

"Henry, in a year you have to press all day and burn all night, get out five thousand, ten thousand a day!"

"Nobody is building that much."

"Because lumber, she too dear!"

He thought of Keefe. What would Keefe say? He knew in his heart what Keefe would say. The smell of money was in it. It was as rich as mules, and less time to wait for the money.

But it seemed that the few softwood trees nearby would not make good kiln-coke, too. Soft coal would have to be hauled from the railroad. "You haul bricks down, coal back. Nobody else got wagon, nobody else got horse. Henry, what if we get big wheat crop next year? Who going haul it? Henry, you keep five wagons busy all year!"

With what he and Elmer called "the bank money," it would be easy. Also, if Elmer had any luck—and any sense—in Grand Island, he should be returning with more than two thousand dollars. They owed twelve hundred of it to the Salcomb Bank, and they still owed Mrs. Reynolds twenty-five hundred. But maybe they could stall somebody.

They got into a buggy and rode into Salcomb and had George Weedy draw up a contract under which Henry and Elmer each owned thirty-five percent of the brickyard, Sedlacek thirty percent. Henry would put up a thousand dollars, with which Louie would go to Omaha and buy the press and coal. Henry and Elmer were also obligated to furnish teams and wagons as needed.

Driving home after leaving the two Bohemians off at the creek in the cool of the evening, Henry did not regret having plunged into the deal. And yet he thought, why do I want money? I eat well. I sleep in my own house. What else is there to want. . . . ?

"A woman like Yvonne Keithly," he said aloud. Sometimes she came back so vividly that his own blood blinded him, and he knew that that slim, pale, quiet little Lillian Brown was never going to be woman enough for him.

He had written to his father, asking for a loan. Bill Ely had replied promptly, enclosing a draft for $1,602.35 and a letter that said:

> My dear son:
>
> A pleasure to hear from you at last. You don't need to borrow. Sold no beef the year you left but horses fetched good money. You and Guillermo entitled to a third of a net of $12,017.70, said share amounting to $4,005.90 each. You went off and left him with all the work, so three parts to him and two to you is fair. So your third comes out $2,403.55 to him and $1,602.35 to you, which I enclose.
>
> Beef a bad proposition here due to drought, so nothing coming to you there. If you have a good investment either Glmo. or I can help. But we are in deep with Chris at the mill. It will

prosper in time, Chris is a good worker and Natalee not a spender, but it takes time.

Glmo. will marry Lura Rhodes. You don't know them. Rhodes is land agt. for the RR, they are cultured people so your mother has companionship. She sends her love, so do Glmo. & Natalee.

I hope you still have Tom Monk. I don't know the mule mkt. but a good stud horse is a good income as well as the mark of a stable & prosperous man. Wd. appreciate hearing about him. I remain affectionately your father, Wm. Ely.

So Billy was getting married, and his sister and her husband had started a mill of some kind! Not a word about the Riordans, who must have been in Bill Ely's mind, and no indication as to whether he would be welcome at home. He did not answer the letter. "Let Tom Monk answer it," he said to Elmer. "It's more his letter than mine."

The Reverend Brown's milk cows were out on the road again. The preacher was like the Riordans, in that he always took on more than he could manage. He got on Henry's nerves a lot, but he was still their neighbor and Lillian's father; so he pushed his team on past his own gate to the Browns, to tell them about their cows.

He never felt really comfortable there, and Lillian drove him crazy. She took fits where she wanted to kiss and kiss until he thought he'd explode, and then suddenly she'd freeze up and practically run him off the place. He felt sorry for Elmer, too. Old Man Brown had bought a good organ, which Louise played by ear until Henry taught her to read music. When the four of them were together, Louise was more interested in the music than in Elmer.

He turned in at the preacher's place, and Louise came to the door. "Why hello, Henry," she said.

"Hidy, Louise. Is your pa at home?"

"No. He went to a convention in Broken Bow, didn't you know?"

"No I didn't." (The old, fool, going away and leaving two girls alone.) "I wanted to tell him that both of your cows are out, is all. I'd run them in except I've got this game leg."

"I turned them out to graze. They'll come home by milking time. Won't you come in, Henry?"

"I reckon not. If you and Lillian need anything, you be sure to holler."

"Lillian's with Daddy. Listen, Henry, did you get your scythe back?"

"I don't think so. (You just bet not! Getting back something that old Brown borrowed was real work.) "You tell your pa I'll pick it up next time."

"No, Daddy's through with it and you'll need it yourself. It's down in the barn."

She ran to the barn with a light skipping step. She was not really fat, just a strong, filled-out woman. It was her severity, something stronger than primness, that gave her that forbidding matronly look.

"I thought it was here," she called from the barn. "Do you know where Daddy keeps things?"

He shook the lines and let the team amble to the barn. He tied them to the ring set in the cornerpost and got out with his cane. It was a big one-story barn with a plank floor, whitewashed inside because Reverend Brown had held services here until the congregation got a church built closer to Salcomb.

The far door was opened. Louise was outlined against the western sun in it, looking around blindly. There was nothing out of the ordinary to cause this sudden breathlessness in Henry as he hobbled toward her, but it was like getting some kind of silent message. She turned to face him, her big, soft, warm mouth half open. When he dropped the cane and held out his arms, she went into them, the next thing, he was pressing kiss after kiss on that eager hungry mouth.

He pulled her deeper into the barn, still kissing her. They went to their knees in the soft hay together.

There was not an ounce of fat on her anywhere. Her waist was as slim as Lillian's. It was those damned shapeless Methodist dresses the old man bought for her.

He spent the night with her in the bed she shared with Lillian, but he slept very little. Louise lay on her side, with one leg across him, sleeping deeply with a contented smile on her relaxed mouth. Henry stared up at the ceiling and tried to sort out his scattered thoughts. He could not remember ever being so confused about himself.

For one thing, he had the feeling of being as much a man as he had to be. There were no doubts in him about Yvonne Keithly now. If a man was man enough, then the woman became womanly. And that had been Keefe's trouble. He had let his woman be the man.

For another thing, he was dead-moral-certain that he was not Louise's first. She was just too good at this, and she enjoyed it too much.

Then there was the way she babbled, "Do you love me, Henry? I loved you from the beginning. I hated Lillian because she got you and I got old dumb Elmer. Did you love me that way, too?"

Before daylight they both awakened hungry. They hurled themselves at each other for a while, and then she got up and ran through the house stark naked, to bring him bacon sandwiches and a big piece of cake and coffee in her father's own oversize mug. She got back in bed and propped herself up on her elbow to watch him eat. Their nakedness somehow gave her an advantage.

"I know what you're thinking," she said.

"What?"

"That you're not my first."

"Well yes, I thought of that."

"You don't like that."

"Well, it's different with a man. A man is a street dog in that respect. He shouldn't be, but he is. A woman risks more. She could have a kid."

"How many kids have you fathered?"

"None, by God!"

"I've never had any either. You don't need to worry, Henry. If I have your baby and you don't want to marry me, you don't have to."

"Oh hell, Louise, I'd marry you!"

"You said you loved me." She wept a little. "I thought you were doing this for love, Henry."

"I guess I do love you. Louise, listen—who was the other man?"

"There were three."

"Three? Good God!"

They were suddenly quarreling. She stopped crying and got out of bed and dressed herself. "Go on home, Henry," she said. "You're more narrow-minded than my father. I really did love you. You're the kind of man I want for a husband. I never met that kind of man before, but I knew what I wanted. I would be a good wife to you. You'd never have to worry about any other man, if that's what you're thinking."

"Good lord, Louise, I wasn't—"

"I know what your trouble is! I'm your first, ain't I? Oh, go on home! I despise you."

"Well, I don't despise you. You're the one who—"

"Look into your own heart, Henry. Oh, it could have been so good for us!"

He did go home eventually, but first there were more degrading, abrading words between them. On the way home, he met Louie Sedlacek plodding along the road in his best clothes, a derby hat, a red shirt, and a swallow-tailed coat. Louie carried a note from Herman Lozik:

> *Hinry figrin and figrin there still ant enuf muny, louie needs 500 to 1000 $ more. Is in hastings brick press make 500 hour. So giv louie 500 or 1000, we bin figrin all nite, cant du with les.*

Henry's mind was on other things. All he thought was that he had better satisfy Louie before he and Herman got to "figrin" again. He left the Bohunk drinking coffee in the kitchen and without a qualm dug up "the bank money" from the dirt floor of Tom Monk's box stall. He handed over a thousand dollars of it almost absentmindedly.

He discarded the cane. The days passed with hobbles on them. Once Reverend Brown stopped by. He was full of enthusiastic ideas, most of which seemed to point toward Henry and Elmer joining the church. He had bought an old wrecked buckboard and shrunk the wheels and tires himself, installed a new reach and hounds, and enameled it green. He had put a green-striped awning over the seat and had bought a pair of bay harness mares.

"For my girls," he said. "They have a rig of their own, and need not go about in a box wagon like a nester family. How do you like it?"

"It's a smart turnout," Henry said. The old preacher could do just about anything—cabinetry, carpentry, blacksmithing, cobble shoes, and above all, make money.

"I don't hold with show or style, but a man should see that his womenfolk live up to his station in life. The nesters take better care of their livestock than they do their wives and daughters."

"They do for sure."

A few days later, Henry saw a spot of green on the county road. He saddled Tom Monk quickly. If it was the reverend again, he did not want to be trapped here in the house. On the other hand, if it was Louise, he could not afford to miss a chance.

It was Louise under the awning, pale and square-jawed as a schoolteacher. Both of her new mares seemed to be in heat, and Tom Monk misbehaved in an embarrassing fashion. Well, let her *be* embarrassed.

He tipped his hat. "Hidy, Louise, how are you?"

"I'll live," she said coldly.

"You look peaked. It's this danged heat."

"It's not the heat," she said contemptuously. "It happened, that's what."

"What happened?"

"Oh I forgot! You're a respectable man. You like to pretend things don't happen. Well, this time they did. I woke up this morning throwing up all over the house." Her voice became a hate-filled squeak. "Are you that ignorant? I'm in the family way!"

"Oh my God, no!" he moaned.

She seemed to get control of herself. "I'd say it was too early to be sure, except for the way my mother was. She could count the day both of us would be born, from her first morning sickness. It's not the first time it happened in the world, but it's going to just break Daddy's heart."

"Louise, you're crying."

"Why wouldn't I? A man gets off scot free, but this is no fun for the woman, believe me!"

Tom Monk reached out and romanced the near mare, taking a bite at her neck. The mare squealed and laid back her ears in a strictly formal display of indignation that fooled no one, least of all Tom Monk.

Henry hauled the stud backward halfway across the road. "You son of a bitch, is that all you think of?"

"How is he different from you?" Louise screamed.

"Goddamn it, that is not fair!"

"Don't you swear at me! It's not fair for me to be knocked up either, but I am."

He slid out of the saddle, tightened the stud's curb chain so he could handle him with the riding reins, and led him to the side of the buggy. "Stand there!" he said, taking a twist of the reins around his left hand. He put his right hand on Louise's knee.

"Let's get married."

"I'd rather be dead than married to you."

"For the baby's sake."

"Ha, you don't even know if it's your baby!"

"Louise! That was a hell of a thing to say. Do I have to get down on my knees and beg you?"

"You never begged for anything in your life, unless it was money."

"At least I take Sunday off. I ain't passing the collection plate every Sunday for it." She's going to make me say it, he thought hopelessly. Well, I will. But I'll do it my own way. . . .

He ran his hand up under her skirt and took hold of one of her firm strong legs, just under the knee. "Goddamn you, I love you, and you're going to marry me!" he shouted.

She came tumbling out of that gaudy buckboard into his arms, crying and laughing and exclaiming, "How can I be so ornery to you when I love you so much? It *is* your baby, Henry—*you* know that. Those other men, one was my cousin and—"

"Shush that!" If she kept on blabbing, she'd soon have it out of him that Riordan's wife was as close as he had ever come, and how she'd laugh if she ever found out how that had turned out!

Elmer came in two hours after sundown with a big freight wagon pulled by four feather-footed Clydesdale mares. Four others ambled behind the wagon with halter ropes tied up under their chins.

"What do you think of 'em?" Elmer crowed. "Used up by a railroad grading gang to McCook. So gimpy I had to change horses every day to keep going, but bring on old Screamer. Won't they throw some fine mules?"

"Elmer, what did they cost you?"

"Hundred and fifty apiece, and ain't one more than eight years old."

"A bargain I wish we could afford."

Elmer paid no attention. "Got a big load of stuff. You wouldn't believe the deal I got on this wagon, too."

He threw back the tarp to show his treasures: a barrel of sugar, two of flour, four big lamps like the ones Ed Clark had in his room at the O Bar O, a green plush sofa, a dozen new railroad shovels, and a tom turkey and four hens.

"They have an auction every week. We kin double our money on all of that stuff."

"Did you bring back any money at all?"

"Right at three hundred."

"Elmer, we're in the brickyard business."

"Good!" Elmer roared. "Listen, I bought a case of whisky too. It's coming on the season that if I want a drink to warm me up, I want it, whether Rev'rend Brown appreciates it or not. Let's turn these plugs into the corral and unload tomorrow. I want a drink. This is the first time I ever owned more than one bottle at a time."

Henry put some beans on to warm and mixed a batch of biscuits. While waiting on the biscuits, he told Elmer about the brickyard.

"Well then, we have to dig into the bank money."

"How can we?" Henry said.

"Ol' buddy, we'll be dealing money and stuff so fast a Philadelphia lawyer couldn't never cipher it out. Henry, listen, I learned one thing in Grand Island. *I learned how you make money!* You just buy low and sell high, that's all."

"I could have told you that."

"Nobody can tell you, Henry. You find it out for yourself, or you don't. I could make money anywhere in the world now, but I thought it over, and I still love this place better than any place I ever been, and I still want you for a partner raising mules."

Henry gripped the edge of the table and said, "Maybe not after I tell you this. Louise and I are in love. We're going to get married."

Elmer cocked his head. "What? Hey! You and Louise? You? And Louise?"

Henry's hand shot across the table and closed on Elmer's big wrist. "Keep your hands in sight, Elmer. You never saw the day you could kill me with any gun ever made. So don't try it!"

They struggled with each other across the table. Henry got the gun and tossed it behind him into the kitchen woodbox. Elmer flung the table out of the way and came at him, shouting, "Then I'll kill you with my bare hands, you doublecrossing Texas son of a bitch!"

"Elmer! I'll shoot you if I have to. Louise is going to have a baby, and she's not going to bring it up without a daddy. *Goddamn you. Elmer—*"

Elmer had snatched up the stove poker and swung it. Henry took it across his back, but it smashed the lamp and the room was filled with light as the flowing kerosene caught fire. Henry yanked the oilcloth off the table and smothered the fire.

Elmer had collapsed into a chair in the corner. "You already got her fixed up. Hell of a homecoming this is."

"Don't tell me I'm a yellow dog, Elmer, because I feel worse than any yellow dog. But this is the only woman I ever met that I'd give up everything else for. I just don't even care what you think."

"But you never liked her!"

"I'm more surprised than you are."

"How did it happen?"

"I just don't know, Elmer. I don't think she does either. Only she did say this, she said she always did like me."

"And all that time I was shining up to her! What gets me, Henry, is all the women you've had and all the women you *could* have, a good-looking educated fellow like you, and you pick on mine."

"Here's where that breaks down. She never was yours. And nobody else knows this, but she's the first woman I ever had in my life."

"Oh, you're a liar!" Then Elmer leaned forward to study Henry closely. "The man that killed Dave Rogers, and you never had a woman before?"

"You finally hit it, Elmer. A killer has got something missing where women are concerned."

"You don't seem to be short anything."

"Not now. But I was."

Elmer drove his fist into the wall. "And I bought them four lamps home, two for you and Lillian and two for Louise and me! Say, does Lillian know?"

"She does by now. Louise wasn't going to tell her, but Louise agrees with me, it won't make any difference to her. Lillian don't care if I freeze to death."

Elmer stormed out of the house and came back with a bottle of whisky from the cases in the wagon. He pulled the cork and, out of habit, offered the bottle first to Henry. Henry shook his head and set the beans and biscuits on the table.

"Listen, did you ever love Lillian up?" Elmer asked.

"Oh lord no! I'd have to say she's as nice a girl as I ever met, but I wouldn't even think of trying to get fancy with her."

Elmer had a drink and then another. He ate lightly, sitting sidewise at the table with his legs crossed and staring into the corner. Suddenly he turned, wrinkling his nose at Henry.

"This place will smell of coal oil for a month," he said. "All right Henry, you get this: I'm going to marry that pretty little Lillian, and build her a brick house with the first bricks out of your goddamn brickyard, and whenever I feel like it, I'm going to take her in there and just love her to death. You can argue with that big stubborn Louise the rest of your life for all I care, but I don't ever want to see you even *look* at Lillian."

"Maybe it was meant to be that way," Henry said.

"It is now, anyhow. I never will smell coal oil again without—without—"

Elmer put his face into his hands and dropped his elbows on the table. A sob like the bawling of a calf came out of him. Elmer would be ashamed of this when he remembered it tomorrow, but not half as ashamed as his best friend felt. Was any woman worth doing this to a friend? And ashamed though he was Henry felt the quick answer in his own heart, This one is. . . .

Chapter Eleven

The early light was in Louise's face, but she slept so soundly that she did not know when he pulled the blanket over her. Thunder rumbled, and a cool draft flowed through the open house as the first raindrops spattered on the window. The oats that Elmer and Daddy Brown had sown were heading out, six hundred acres of them, pasture for the mares and the mule colts that were starting to arrive, and a wealth of winter feed.

My father-in-law, Henry thought, watching the rain, has influence in the right places. . . . There was work to do, but Louise's time was near, and these rich, lazy mornings in the bedroom would soon be over.

The rain hit hard suddenly. Louise stirred. "Go back to sleep!" he whispered. "The Lord came through for your dad again, and for those who own the land next to his."

It was June and they were old married folks. Elmer and Lillian had married on Thanksgiving, and were living with Daddy Brown. Lillian's time would be in August. Elmer and the reverend got along fine.

Sheet lightning flared, and a gust of cold wind made the curtains stand out straight. Henry got up and plodded naked about the house, checking all points of the compass for a tornado formation. He saw a four-horse team coming up the road, pulling a wagon stripped down to running-gears and loaded with bags of coal for their brick kilns.

Another wagon followed, carrying lumber to frame in the big brick house Elmer was building for Lillian. One of us, Henry thought, is going to have to give in here, and it'll have to be Elmer. I've got the most money tied up in this deal. . . .

On the surface, nothing had changed, and Elmer probably thought sincerely that this was the case. But Elmer had got a taste of managing, of making money. And whether he believed it or not, there was still a sore spot in him about Louise.

The four dogs—Louise was one of those women who liked plenty of dogs watching the place—set up a foofaraw. Henry pulled on his pants and stepped into his boots. Bare from the belt up, he went to the door.

It was his father-in-law in the awninged buckboard, with side curtains now too, and a stranger was seated beside him. Sheriff Omicron Deal was riding that big flashy sorrel that he called Chester A. Arthur. It could not have rained any harder on Noah than it was raining now. Henry waved and pointed.

"Pull right into the barn! I'll be right down."

He remembered that his slicker was in the barn. He ran out half naked, and closed the barn doors behind all of them. The three men had all dismounted.

"This is not a social call," Reverend Brown said. "General, my son-in-law, Henry Ely. Henry, General Aaron Palmer. Henry, Omi and the general want to talk to you, but first, I picked this up in town for you this morning."

He handed Henry a letter. Henry shook hands with General Palmer, a white-haired, white-bearded man as wide as he was tall, and the sheriff. He excused himself to read his letter. Dr. Joseph S. Littlejohn was answering Henry's long-ago appeal for money at last.

But from Sacramento? He opened the letter and saw what looked like a draft or check—something on pink bond paper. He kept it hidden in the envelope while he read Doc's letter:

> Friend Jack-Henry whichever it is:
>
> Your letter arrived via Pueblo, New York, San Francisco, and Stockton. Hope it is not too late for us to be of assistance to you. I employ

the plural because I have had the extreme good fortune to have married Yvonne Keithly. I practice medicine here, but managing our investments require so much time that I have taken in a partner and plan to turn the practice over to him. The new developments in the healing art cause me to abandon it with regret, but man is the victim of his own good fortune at times.

You asked to borrow $1,500. It happens we have just cashed in some property and have $3,200 to invest. It was our joint inspiration to offer it to you, at 8 percent. You are sure to be a wealthy man, but you traders always attempt more than you plan, thus we are sure you can use the extra.

We leave it to you to send us a proper promissory note. This is not sentiment, friend Jack-Henry, but mere appreciation of your character. Mrs. Littlejohn joins me in sending most affectionate regards and asks me to say that she remembers you most kindly.

As ever your friend,
Jos. S. Littlejohn.

That bitch, Henry thought—oh that wicked, tormented bitch! Poor, miserable, infatuated Doc, who had the fatal defect of being a gentleman, and who would not slap her around as she needed and wanted to be slapped around. He'll end up crying in his pillow or taking a whole bottle of pills, but I wonder if it won't be worth it to him.

"What's on your mind, men?"

Sheriff Deal said, "Henry, there's a mix-up of some kind here. General Palmer runs the Ripley National Bank up there by the Dakota line.

Henry seemed to have been waiting for this for a long time, but he looked at Palmer and said, "The bank that was robbed last year. I was through there at that time."

"Right!" Palmer said. "I have information that you may be able to help us with that case. It was a brilliant operation, just brilliant! But we have had some luck that takes us part of the way, and we hope you can assist us the rest of the way. We lost nearly thirteen thousand dollars—twelve thousand, nine hundred and eighty dollars, to be exact."

His speech was pure Kentucky—and had not J. A. Tracy, president of the bank, been a Kentuckian? Tracy had not impressed Jack Neely, but General Palmer looked like no fool to Henry Ely. Yet, what was he talking about, $12,980 gone in that stickup? The correct amount, $8,320, was engraved forever in Henry's brain.

He said, "I ran into the posse as I was leaving Ripley. The idea I got, they were scared stiff they might blunder into that gang, but I could be wrong about them. How can I help?"

Sheriff Deal said, "Henry, the general has the idea that you was one of the holdup men."

"Idea, hell," said Palmer. "I have information."

"I held up that bank?" Henry said. "I did?"

"I have that information."

"You better have, coming on my place with that kind of talk."

"Did you ever use the name of Jack Neely? Did you kill a man by the name of Dave Rogers, and—"

Henry cut in angrily, "What has this got to do with your bank? The sheriff knows I ran as Jack Neely for a while. I collected a reward for killing Rogers."

"Did you kill a man by the name of Oliver Pierce—Buster, he was called?" General Palmer went on in a rush. "Did you ever wear a moustache? Did you ever know two men by the names of Owen Simington and Marcus Peek? Did you turn two old unbranded nags loose on the Flying Y, south of Ripley, and burn a wagon and tarp there?"

"Answer him, Henry," Reverend Brown said furiously. "Answer General Palmer."

There was only one person who could have given out this kind of information—only one person sneaky enough. It was that girl-faced ninny of a Peek. They had caught Peek, and he had tried to skin out by throwing the blame on everyone else. But not twelve thousand dollars' worth! Where had that figure come from?

Henry looked at his father-in-law. "What does Elmer say about this?"

"Thank the lord, Elmer and Lillian don't know about it. They left early this morning to go to Ogallala to get Lillian a harness mare." The preacher shook his finger in Henry's face. "Defend yourself, Henry. Let's hear you defend yourself if you can!"

"Oh shut up," Henry said. "General, let's hear you accuse me out-and-out, Goddamn you."

"Ely, the best detective in the bank business has worked on this case ever since it happened," Palmer said. "You don't think I'm going to let somebody clean me out of ten thousand dollars and just sit on my butt, do you? I am like hell. We got about thirty-one hundred of it back. I look around me here, at a mighty prosperous place, and by God it seems to me that some of my bank's money is in it!"

"Then why don't you arrest me?"

(They had got back thirty-one hundred, had they? Were *both* Marcus Peek and Owen Simington caught? And what about Old Elmer? Nobody had mentioned his name yet.)

"I'm sheriff of Ripley County," Palmer said, "but I'm a fair man. I don't want to arrest anybody and then regret it. I want you to square yourself.

"But there's something here that don't ring true, it just don't! I'll tell you how far I'll go with you to be fair. You come to Ripley with me and straighten this out, and if I'm wrong, I'll pay you ten thousand dollars in character damages. I keep my promises. But if I am wrong, by God I want the ten thousand that is due me, and I'll get it."

It was the end of the world. This old Kentucky booger knew just how to get at a man. But I want to know how that loot got to be four thousand dollars too big, Henry thought, and I want somebody to say something that'll let me know where Elmer stands in this proposition. . . .

"Am I under arrest, General?"

"Why, I reckon not. If I can get a horse somewhere, we can start back now and camp wherever we play out, and be there tomorrow. I'm not as young as I once was, but I want this cleaned up."

"Fair enough. I do, too," Henry said. "You pick yourself out a horse and let me get dressed."

Louise was pulling on the shirt and overalls she wore to take care of her chickens and garden. It had stopped raining, and he knew by the look on her face that she was in one of those frenzies to make the dirt fly. "If you want chickens," he had told her, "you take care of them. I'd rather buy eggs."

"What does Daddy want, in this weather?" she asked.

He wanted to take her hands; but better not. "Louise, remember about that bank holdup in Ripley? The fellow that runs that bank, he's the sheriff of the county there too, and he's got the idea I was one of that gang that stuck up that bank."

"You are? They think you stuck up a bank?"

He got a waterproof valise out of the closet and began throwing clothes into it. "I told him I'd go up there and settle it. You better put up some kind of grub for two. We're leaving right away."

"In this rain?"

"It has let up."

"You wait a minute here, Henry." She came around in front of him as he scrambled for clean socks and a shirt. "Daddy didn't accuse you, did he? What would Daddy know about it?"

"Not knowing anything never stopped him yet from giving his opinion. He has done found me guilty, Louise."

There was a long silence. Her hands went to her cheeks and she said, "You did it. Oh God, my baby's going to have a thief for a daddy."

"Well say, my family sure does stand by me!"

"You did it. You know you did! They couldn't drag you up there if you hadn't done it. Don't make it any worse by denying it. Don't be a liar as well as a thief."

"Louise, I'll take that from you just once—"

She was suddenly in perfect control of herself. "Oh Henry, do you think I'm a fool? I know what it is to do a thing, knowing it's the wrong thing at the time, yet doing it anyway. That's what sin is—not what you do, but knowing it's wrong. And you know it, too."

Indeed he did. He remembered planning that robbery,

knowing it was wrong as he did it, yet doing it anyway. So that was what sin was!

"Louise, let me straighten this out."

"Oh sure."

"I can do it. I can straighten it out."

"I don't doubt that a bit. I'll stick. I won't have it said I left you when you were in trouble. But you wait until after this baby is born! I swear to God it's not going to grow up in the house of a thief."

He got his gun out of the closet. It used to hang on a nail in the kitchen, but Louise had started to break him of this habit, for the baby's sake.

"Louise, there's something mighty wrong with this whole proposition, but your mind is made up and there's no use trying to talk to you now."

"There sure ain't. Don't try to justify it! Henry, you've got to pay for what you do wrong in this world. I know!"

Those men she had loved before him—would she never get them off her mind, and let him forget them? He said, "Goddamn it, do you think I'm not paying? I don't beat my breast the way the Browns do, but do you think I've had a waking minute that this hasn't been in the back of my mind? But you get this and get it good, woman, because this is how it is:

"Neither the law, nor your pious old daddy, nor you, nor even the baby, can make me own up to what I never did. After that baby comes, there had better be no talk, in the family or out, making me guilty of more than I did."

"The baby won't even know about you. I won't be here when you get back—if you ever do."

He walked out, sick at heart but thinking, Not twelve thousand dollars, no sir! Somebody sweetened that pot good. . . .

"Good-looking stallion," General Palmer said, as Henry saddled Tom Monk. "Kentucky blood?"

"His sire was Castle."

"And Castle was—let's see, I know he was by Inheritor, out of a McKinstry mare, but which one?"

"You know more about him than I do."

"I tried to buy him as a two-year-old."

"I see."

"I was outbid. McKinstry made a fortune out of Inheritor. I imagine this horse has done well by you."

Henry looked at his father-in-law. "When Elmer gets back, tell him I said nothing is as important as the brood mares. Tell him I want him to be here early and late every day, and keep track of those mule colts as they drop. Tell him if I catch him up there at Ripley, instead of tending to business here, there's going to be an accounting."

"I don't imagine Elmer will have to be reminded of his duty," Reverend Brown said.

Well I do hope you're right for once, Henry thought. I can't have that old loud-mouth on my hands too. . . . He could just hear Elmer squalling at the top of his voice, "Twelve thousand dollars? Are you plumb loco? 'Twasn't but eighty-three twenty!" The thought made his blood run cold.

Chapter Twelve

"You're so good with figures," Henry said, "let's figure it this way. Take it for granted that what you've got is not one man's share of the booty, but two. Let's say—"

"We don't have to take anything for granted," the detective said. "I was a bank examiner for years. The amount missing is very close to four times the amount we recovered from this man. Now that I have met you, Ely, I understand the military precision with which this plan was executed. I always know when I have got my man, and I think I can prove I have him this time."

"One thing," Henry said. "The bank stayed open. Who put up the money to make the books balance, after that robbery?"

"I did," said General Palmer.

"Why not Mr. Tracy?"

"It is my bank, my reputation that was at stake."

"Who is this fellow Tracy?"

The detective, whose name was Harrison, said, "Ely, just what are you getting at?"

"You don't want to take anything for granted, but I'm going to ask you to try it just once. Let's say that what those bandits got away with was about eighty-three hundred dollars—"

"Why that particular sum?"

"Harrison, do me a favor and just keep that figure in mind for a minute. That figure would leave forty-six hundred and sixty dollars unaccounted for. If I were one of those bank robbers, why, right about now I would be wondering where the hell that money went."

Harrison frowned at General Palmer and then back at Henry. The detective was a smooth, well-dressed, clean-shaven man, but under his looks Henry felt a rough one. He already knew everything there was to know about both Henry Ely and Jack Neeley. Oh my yes, really rough inside!

"You would ask Mr. Tracy about that forty-six hundred and sixty dollars, is that it?" the rough one said.

"If I were a robber, I would."

"Ely, Mr. Tracy is General Palmer's brother-in-law, married to his sister. He's from a very fine family. Today he's at home ill—"

"Real bad ill?"

"Not seriously, we hope. Why?"

"The day they bring in the fellow you say robbed his bank, he's home with a slight illness. He saw the whole robbery. He talked with the leader, the fellow you say was me. Why isn't he here to identify me?"

General Palmer said, "Hell's bells, Harrison, why don't you write them figgers down and go ask J.A. about them? Let's get it over with. I've had two strenuous days."

Henry thought, You have indeed . . .! They had pounded up here fast, spending less than five hours in overnight camp. I don't like him and I don't trust him, but there is one tough old Kentucky rooster. . . .

"If you insist," Harrison said, "but I have my own methods."

"I don't insist, but let's twirl or get off the piano stool. Either this man robbed my bank or he didn't. You were so damn sure a few days ago."

"Maybe the reason he's not so sure now is that he didn't go into the books *before* the robbery," Henry said. "Or how do we know what they show since then? How honest is this bank, anyway?"

Harrison got up and went to the window and turned his back. The new Ripley County Courthouse stood on a slope, with the sheriff's office in the rear, on the downhill side. The general and Henry had come in the front door, however, and up some back stairs to the county treasurer's office.

Henry thought he knew why. They were not ready to bring him and Marcus Peek face to face yet. First, Harrison wanted a chance to break Henry down.

It was not yet dark, but it was raining hard, and lamps had been lighted throughout the courthouse. Harrison turned suddenly, a little .32 revolver in his hand. He said, "You're under arrest, Ely. I'm charging you with the robbery of the bank. Anything you say may be used against you."

"This is a doublecross," Henry said.

"No. You came here to clear yourself. Instead, you're trying to throw the blame on the president of the bank. Please stand up. I know your reputation with a gun. I want you to remove yours and put it on the desk beside the lamp, holster and all. If you make one move I don't like, I shall kill you."

Henry stood up, removed his gun belt, and put it on the table. General Palmer reached for it, wrapped the belt around the holster, and put it in his lap. He said, "Ely, this wasn't my idea, but you've still got a chance to clear yourself."

"Let's have the other fellow up here now, and get this over with," the detective said.

Palmer sat near the door, with his chair tipped back against the wall. He turned his head and shouted down the stairs, "Walt! Let's have that prisoner up here now."

Two stories down, a steel door clanged. Two men plodded slowly up two echoing flights of stairs. Henry shouted, *"What the hell here!"* and surged his full weight against the table as the two men came into the room. It was not young Marcus Peek who shuffled in ahead of the deputy sheriff, but old Owen Simington.

Owen looked to be a little closer to death, but not much. His eyes drifted past Henry's and came to rest about a foot above Henry's head. Harrison pointed to Henry.

"Simington, do you know this man?"

"I haven't got anything to say," Owen said wearily. "It won't do any good to ding at me. I ain't ever going to have anything to say."

"How about you, Ely. Know this man?"

Henry said, "I check."

"What does that mean?"

"It means go ahead and fill your hand!" (Oh, he thought, I only hope Owen gets what I'm saying. . . .) "I say only eighty-three hundred and twenty dollars was taken in that robbery. You say nearly thirteen thousand. You don't expect him to own up to somebody else's thievery too, do you? Maybe he wants to know the same thing I'm asking—*where the hell is that forty-six hundred and sixty dollars*?"

His eyes met Owen's briefly, and he knew the doomed old man got the message. But instead of guts and relief and gratitude, what he saw in Owen's look was hatred and fear. Why?

The truth did not hit him suddenly. It fought its way up through the easygoing credulities he had acquired since becoming Henry Ely again. He had to remember being Jack Neely, to understand how things could be.

"I'll make a deal," he said.

"No deals," said Harrison, quickly.

"This one is with General Palmer. General, forty-six hundred and sixty dollars of that money was missing before the robbery. Get that through your head!"

"You are accusing my brother-in-law of embezzlement. No other man could have done it."

"I'm sorry, but there is no other explanation."

"Go on. What's your deal?"

"You say you recovered thirty-one hundred from this man. But you can't claim it for the bank unless you convict him of the robbery, isn't that right?"

"Go on, I'm listening."

"Here's what I'll do. You let Harrison dig into the books of this bank *before* the robbery, and go over Tracy's personal accounts. I am this sure that if nothing is wrong there, I'll plead guilty to the stickup."

"And if something is wrong?"

"We make a deal. Tracy is your banker. You stand the loss for the forty-six hundred and sixty. I'll break this man Simington down right now, so you can claim that for the bank. Now your books show you're short how much today?"

"I have told you already, Twelve thousand, nine hundred and eighty dollars."

"Give me a pencil, somebody. Look—here's the deal I'll make you, General."

Harrison stepped closer, so he could read the figures too, but Henry could feel the .32 in his ribs as General Palmer and the detective studied the paper that Henry slid across the table:

Total loss	$12,980
By embezzlement	4,660
By robbery	$ 8,320
Recovered on Simington	3,100
Balance still missing	$ 5,220
I'll pay now:	3,200
Balance by my note	$ 2,020

"I see!" Palmer scratched his white head. "And I'll bet you walk out with a suspended sentence!"

"No. I walk out clean as a whistle. Nobody files charges on me. I'm innocent!"

Palmer gasped. "I'll be a son of a bitch if you haven't got your gall with you! You come in here and rob my bank, and now you offer me a promissory note to square it, just like that."

"Not all of it. I'll square what I have to square, but not a cent more. Will you prosecute your brother-in-law? You just bet you won't! He'll slide out clean. General, if you weren't suspicious of him before, you sure as hell are now. But you still won't have any family scandal.

"Well I feel the same way. I've got a family, too. No scandal for you, no scandal for us. That's the way it works."

"Let me see if I understand you. You'd buy your way out by turning your own sidekick in?" Harrison asked.

"Or we stand trial together, and you'll never convict us. And when we walk out of here, you owe me ten thousand dollars. I don't expect to collect it from you, but you'll go to your grave owing it to me. And I want to see your face when you have to let Simington walk out of here with that thirty-one hundred!"

Henry hit the table with his fist. "It is this simple—cover for Tracy, and you cover for me too!"

Palmer looked up at Harrison. "We can't convict them if they shut up, can we?" Harrison did not answer. Palmer went on, "How about my brother-in-law, is there enough in the books to convict him?"

Harrison sighed and said nothing. "You leave me no choice," Palmer said to the detective. Still Harrison did not answer. "If you had reason to believe Tracy was robbing me, why didn't you say so?"

Harrison said, "One case at a time, General. I was hired to settle a robbery, not get into a Kentucky family feud. You skin your own skunks."

Palmer studied the paper again. "All right, Mr. Ely, you've got a deal."

Henry took Doc Littlejohn's draft from his pocket. "There's thirty-two hundred. Fix up a thirty-day note for the balance and I'll sign it, and I'll pick it up before it matures."

"Oh, I am sure of that. Now how about the money we took off Simington?"

Henry said, "Owen, this is the dirtiest job I ever had in my life, but you let yourself in for it, not me."

"You dirty son of a bitch," Simington said.

"That's right. That's how I feel, and it's how a man deserves to feel every time he lets himself in for this kind of deal. My wife was telling me about sin this morning. It's doing something you know is wrong, yet going ahead and doing it anyway. When I remember a sick old man with a wife and five kids, I'll be damned if I can blame you for robbing a bank.

"But how much did you ever send them? Not much, I'll bet. Not a cent, probably, because you might have to explain where you got it. You had to get hoggish, too, didn't you? The money meant too much, and that poor dumb Peek kid's share was too easy to get, wasn't it? What did you do, Owen—shoot him in the back?"

Only a crazy man would have jumped a deputy sheriff with a .45 in his belt, but Owen turned and jumped the one behind him. He got the deputy in the crotch with his knee. The deputy screamed with pain, but he clutched Owen by the neck and tried to get at his gun. Owen came down with his knee in the deputy's temple.

Henry snatched the holstered gun from General Palmer's lap. Owen got his hands on the deputy's gun and backed out of the door. Henry went after him, just as Owen turned in the middle of the stairs and began running, but he could not make himself shoot to kill. He squeezed one off and saw it splinter the wooden step between Owen's feet.

The detective hit Henry with his left elbow and knocked him aside. He stepped calmly out into the narrow hall and started quickly but silently down the stairs, his little .32 extended at arm's length. He went out of sight, and then they heard his voice.

"Drop it!"

A .45 blasted twice downstairs. The detective's little .32 cracked just once. Henry was halfway down the stairs, his own gun in his hand, when Harrison came to meet him. The detective looked sick enough to throw up any minute; but not as sick as Henry would have been, had he been the one to kill Simington.

General Palmer crooked his finger at Henry. "You don't mean to start back tonight, do you?" he said. "Plenty of room at my place, and you've got a tired horse."

"I'll take it easy. I know what he can stand, and I've got a wife whose time is on her."

"You owe me two thousand and twenty dollars. Suppose you give me a note for a thousand, and that horse."

"Thanks, General, I can't."

"Just forget the note, then. I would have paid two thousand for that horse's sire as a three-year-old."

"I can't spare him. Without him, I would be something less than I am, and right now I need all the moral support I can find. You know what I mean."

"What do you think I need? My only sister's husband! Mr. Ely, for your sake, I hope you never make so much money that your acts of kindness destroy those you want to help. This is on my conscience."

"Try sticking up a bank once," Henry said.

Halfway home he heard riders coming toward him from the south, riding hard. He pushed Tom Monk off the road and slid out of the saddle to hold the horse's nostrils, to keep him from calling the other horses.

Three men rode past, the one in the lead a big, round-shouldered fellow who was growing a gut, and who slouched in the saddle with a silhouette Henry would have known on the darkest night. He shouted, and they did not hear him. He let go of Tom Monk's nose, and the stud threw up his head and screamed a challenge, and the three riders pulled their horses to a sprawling stop.

"Elmer! Where you headed for?"

Elmer trotted his panting horse back through the dark. "What you doing here, Henry? Listen, they give you any trouble about that dad-blamed bank? How come you figure me to stay home and birth a bunch of damn mules, huh?" he bellowed.

"Sh-h! There's no trouble," Henry said.

"There damn well better not be. I's in that as much as you. They treat you bad back there, Henry? They cain't do that to us, now! You tell us who done it, and we hang his Goddang porch on a steeple."

"Sh-h! Elmer, who are these people?"

"You all right for sure?" Elmer threw his thick leg over the saddle horn. "You ain't on the dodge?"

"No. I wish you'd—"

"Don't you worry about these boys, Henry. I knowed these boys a long time. Them and you and me, we can tip that town of Ripley up and watch it slide off the other edge, we have to. I used to ride with these boys—oh, long before I worked for the O Bar O. They's raising themselves some calves over in Custer County now. Married and settled down, but we can still wring out a wet sock if somebody dares us."

"Elmer, where's Louise's old man? What did you tell him?"

"He's to home. I told him stay to home and look after them mule colts. Somebody's got to."

"And you were headed for Ripley?"

"That's where you was in trouble, wasn't it? What the hell you expect a man to do, Henry?"

I've got myself a partner for sure, Henry thought. I never will be rid of this big loud-mouth now. . . . It was the best feeling he had had all day.

Chapter Thirteen

"I'm going to get Lillian," he said.

"You're not doing any such thing," said Louise.

"Then what do you want me to do?"

"Just get out of here and stay out."

"Honey, what you're having is labor pains, and you—"

"Don't tell me! If you want to do something, go harness a team to the buggy. An easy team."

"To the buggy? Now listen, where do you think you're going?"

Another pain hit her. She stiffened in the rocker, threw back her head, and screamed, "Oh! Oh! Oh!" The pain passed. She mopped the sweat from her face with the cloth she carried. "Into town, to a doctor, where do you think?"

"You'll never make it, honey. You'll have that baby in the buggy beside the road."

"Better than having it here."

"In your own house?"

"I haven't got any house. This is a thief's house and I won't live here. Oh! Oh! Oh!"

He slid down with his back against the wall, to rest on his heels. He held both arms out to her. "Louise, I beg you, just listen and try to understand. That's all over! I'm in the clear."

"You bought your way out."

"I did like hell."

"When I needed you most, you were in jail."

"That's a lie and you know it! I never was in jail, I told you that."

"I don't even know your real name."

"That's another lie."

"Oh! Oh! Oh dear Saviour I can't stand this," she screamed.

He shot to his feet. "I'm going to get Lillian, I don't care what you say."

"That nitwit, what can she do?" Louise locked her legs together and bent over and clutched at her crotch. "It's too late, anyway. Just help me to the bed, Henry."

He raged at her as he picked her up, "Fifty of the last sixty hours on a horse, and the minute I'm home you go completely insane."

"There's a brand-new oilcloth in the second drawer in the kitchen. Put it on the bed. Don't bother with the sheet. Put it right on top of it."

"What the hell do you want with an oilcloth?"

Then he saw that she was dribbling all over his bare arm, and he lost his wits. He let her sink to the floor, and terror gripped him as she lowered herself all the way to her knees. "Oilcoth!" she gasped, and he ran to the kitchen and got it, a new white one, and spread it on the bed.

"Now put a sheet on top of it."

"Sweetheart, where in the hell are they?"

"Where they always are."

"Oh, sure. . . ."

He got the oilcloth covered with a sheet and helped her off with her dress, which was all she had on. She was quite calm now, although gray pale and sweaty, with ghastly gray circles around her eyes.

"Now go out and close the door, but wait in the living room. It's too late to go for anyone, but I may need some help. And don't be scared. I've helped at lots of childbirths!"

"Oh sure you have, in a pig's ass!"

"Well three. It's perfectly natural and I'm healthy as a cow, but I'll need you to help cut the cord afterward and—and so forth. The scissors and some rags to tie with are in a pot on the stove. Oh, and wash your hands, Henry."

He went out, and she got up and closed the door behind

him. He heard her moaning, but the moment he touched the doorknob she screamed at him. He went into the kitchen and got out a bottle of the whisky that Elmer had not dared to take with him when he went to live with their father-in-law.

He pulled the cork and drank from the bottle. He heard Louise yelp like a dog. He sprinted for the bedroom.

"Get out, get out!" she screamed at him, when he opened the door. He closed the door, and she called in a somewhat gentler voice, "Better be patient, Henry. It will be some time yet."

He put the bottle down in the living room and got out the old harmonica he had dragged around over six or eight states. He played "Lorena" and "Seventh Regiment Bluejackets" and then some of the hymns Louise liked. He saw his father-in-law drive into the yard and tie his team to the front gatepost, and he thought, Just let him start something. Just let him . . .!

Reverend Brown came in without knocking, a privilege he always claimed. Henry said, "Sit down and be comfortable. Louise's time is on her."

"And you drinking and playing music. Oh my stars, I'll go get Lillian!"

"Louise won't have her. She says Lillian is a nitwit."

"She is at that. What can I do then, Henry?"

"Better have some nerve medicine, Daddy Brown. It's what a doctor would tell you to do."

"I'm sure you're right this time, Henry." The preacher smiled wanly and went into the kitchen for a glass. He poured himself a strong medicinal drink and got it down. "In a little while I will feel better, but I feel like vomiting now," he said.

"It works the other way round with me."

"How did you make out in Ripley?"

"All clear, Daddy Brown."

"What do you mean by that?"

"Just what I said. Ask General Palmer. He and I got along fine, although he was a little put out when I wouldn't sell him my horse."

A piercing scream came from the bedroom. Reverend Brown put his glass down, fell into the rocker, closed his eyes and began to pray. Henry was into the bedroom before Louise could protest—and indeed she did not even try.

"Help me up onto my knees so I can get hold of the bedstead. It's coming sooner than I thought and I want to hold onto something."

"No, lay down there and hold onto my hands, sweetheart. *Goddamn* it, why didn't you let me call Lillian or somebody?"

Healthy as a cow, she had said, and that's just what it made Henry think of, a cow dropping an oversize calf. The same blood and slime. The same bubbling noises, the same grunting and groaning. The same spooky kicking from that blood-covered little thing that had got itself born alive.

For his baby had come into the world.

"It's a boy, Louise," he said.

She crouched on her knees, picked it up by the heels, and whacked its bottom to make it cry. It strangled once, got the birth-phlegm out, and blatted like a lamb. Henry brought the boiled scissors and the boiled rags. He tied the cord in two places the way she showed him, and then made the cut between them.

Louise cleaned out almost immediately, like a good old cow that had been doing this all her life. He wrapped all that junk up in the oilcloth and took it outside and poured kerosene on it and burned it. He brought the bottle of castor oil and the soft rags, and in a few minutes the baby was ready to be shown to its grandfather.

"What did you tell him about the bank?" she whispered.

"Nothing. He—"

"Don't tell him anything. It's none of his business. Henry, I'm sorry I cursed you."

"I had it coming."

"But the Lord says, 'Judge not, lest ye be judged.' Just so we're never ashamed again, either one of us. We both know how it feels."

Reverend Brown came in to inspect his first grandson. "Oh my, isn't he a big one!"

Louise cuddled Henry's hand to her cheek. "I think we'll keep him."

"Congratulations, Henry. What are you going to name him?"

"The way he's built," Louise said, pointing, "we ought to call him Tom Monk."

"Louise!" her father choked, when he got it.

"Why I thought for both grandfathers," said Henry. "William Amos Ely."

The old preacher flushed with pride. "Why not Amos William? It's more euphonic. Amos William Ely, doesn't that come easier to the tongue? Try the initials, A. W. Ely, why a quite distinguished signature."

"It's all right with me," Henry said, thinking, shit, I can't even name my own kid! But when I look back at the start I got—those Riordans, Dave Rogers, that Yvonne woman, Buster Pierce, and that bank—when you come right down to it, and I'm having a whole lot more luck than I really deserve. . . .